How To
Forgive A
Highlander

The MacGregor Lairds

How To
Forgive A
Highlander

The MacGregor Lairds

Michelle
McLean

Entangled Publishing, LLC
2614 South Timberline Road
Suite 105, PMB 159
Fort Collins, CO 80525
rights@entangledpublishing.com

Scandalous is an imprint of Entangled Publishing, LLC.

Edited by Erin Molta
Cover design by EDH Graphics
Cover photography from PeriodImages and DepositPhotos

Manufactured in the United States of America

First Edition July 2019

SCANDALOUS

To Erin, who changed my life with a phone call.

Chapter One

Rose Thatcher's eyes scanned the horizon, looking for any signs of a dead body. So far, no luck. Not that she hoped he was dead. But considering the bullheaded fool had already been wounded when he'd led a pack of their enemies out into the wilderness, it seemed more than likely. She ignored the rush of sadness and regret the thought of William MacGregor's demise brought her. It was nothing but guilt stemming from the clod's somewhat noble sacrifice.

Young Rob, the groom her mistress's kinsman had insisted on sending with her, rode silently beside her, though she could almost feel him working up the courage to complain again. They were several hours from Glenlyon and Kirkenroch, homes of the MacGregor lairds. Rob didn't think that William could have traveled so far, wounded as he was. Rose knew better. William was as stubborn as they came. He wouldn't have upped and died close to home. No. He would have crawled to his hiding place on his hands and knees, if necessary, just to make life more inconvenient for her.

That might be a little unfair. Then again, he'd done worse.

"Miss," Rob said. "I think if we havena found him yet…"

"We'll find him," she said, as she'd said every time he'd uttered the same nonsense.

She had to find him. She owed him.

He'd saved her life more than once. True, her life wouldn't have been in danger if he hadn't kidnapped her in the first place. But she had to grudgingly admit that once he'd realized his mistake, he'd done everything he could to keep her safe.

So. She would find him. Save him. Bring him home. And then they could go their separate ways.

She wouldn't allow herself to think of any other outcome. Not finding him, or finding him dead—that hurt too much to contemplate.

Finding him, saving him, and then walking away… Would that hurt even more?

She kicked her horse into a trot, trying to banish all thoughts from her mind. It seemed no matter how this search ended, she would be in the same boat.

Damn William. She cursed the day he'd ever laid eyes on her.

• • •

Dover, England, Three Weeks Earlier

Rose sucked in a deep breath, her nose wrinkling against the stench of fish and unwashed bodies. The docks were bustling with activity, even so early in the morning. Under normal circumstances, she might have been fascinated to watch the comings and goings of the sailors, fishmongers, dockworkers, and other strange people who frequented the docks. But today was not a normal day.

She handed her mistress, Lady Alice Chivers, her carrying case with a sense of foreboding that twisted her stomach into knots.

"Are you sure this is what you want to do, my lady? It's not too late to turn back."

Lady Alice gave her a fond smile. "Of course, I'm sure! I'm finally free. And in a few more minutes, I'll be safely aboard the ship and on the way to my new life. Safe and sound. You worry far too much, Rose."

In her opinion, Lady Alice didn't worry enough. She was far from safe and sound.

"But, my lady, what if Mr. MacGregor doesn't appear? What if he changed his plans and is sailing on a different ship? Or not sailing at all? Are you sure you can trust him?"

Lady Alice's smile faltered for a split second. "Of course I can trust him. He and his ilk are all about their honor. He wouldn't lie to a lady. Not with the information I am holding over him, in any case. If he goes back on his word, I'll betray him to the authorities as an associate of the Highland Highwayman and have him arrested."

"Would you really?"

Lady Alice rolled her eyes. "Of course not. But he doesn't know that."

Rose frowned, and Lady Alice laughed and pulled her into a smothering embrace. "Oh, you dear thing. Don't worry so! Everything is going according to plan. We've made it all the way here, and I'll be onboard and out to sea before anyone realizes I'm gone. I can't wait to see the look on Mr. MacGregor's face when he finds me on the ship."

Rose didn't share her lady's enthusiasm, but there was no stopping Lady Alice once she got a notion in her head.

"My lady, if you insist on doing this, please let me accompany you. My place is with you."

"My dear, sweet Rose. I would love nothing more than to bring you with me. But I have need of you here. And I know how much you would hate Scotland," she said, patting Rose's cheek.

She wasn't wrong. If Rose had her way, she'd never step foot out of London. She'd certainly never travel to the remote and barbaric Highlands of Scotland. The thought of her mistress doing so filled her with dread and sorrow. But if Lady Alice were going, then Rose wanted to be at her side. No matter where that took her.

But she would obey her mistress's orders.

"Now, you remember what you are to do, yes?" Lady Alice asked.

Rose nodded. "Once the ship is out of sight, I'm to go back to the inn and wait in your chamber. If anyone should come looking for you, I'm to say that you aren't feeling well and would like your meals sent to the room and to turn away all visitors for as long as possible. Tomorrow, I will tell your parents that I discovered you missing and give them the note you left in your room."

"Excellent." Lady Alice beamed at her and then glanced back at the ship. "All right, then. I suppose I should be going. The sun will rise soon, and I wish to be firmly ensconced in my quarters before Mr. MacGregor arrives."

"My lady..." Rose tried again, but Lady Alice shushed her and pulled her into another hug.

"Thank you for all your help, Rose." She kissed her on the cheek and cupped her face in her hands. "You have always been more than a maid to me. You are my true, dear friend, and I shall miss you terribly."

She crushed her in another embrace and then released her and marched toward the ship with a jaunty bounce in her step. To Lady Alice, she was about to embark on a wondrous adventure. To Rose, her lady was making the worst mistake of her life.

She could only pray that all went according to plan and that her mistress would be safe. But the crushing weight in the pit of her stomach made her fear what the future would bring.

• • •

William MacGregor helped his cousin Philip unload the supplies from the wagon, but his attention remained on the bustling activity around them. The docks teemed with people from all walks of life. It would be easy for a spy to slip in among them. Someone who might recognize Philip as one of the MacGregors of Glenlyon. Who might pass that information along to their greatest enemy, Fergus Campbell. Or Ramsay, as he now called himself.

William had spent the better part of a year in enemy territory, doing what he could to keep his kin and clan safe. He would feel much better once Philip was safely aboard the ship and on his way back to Scotland.

William climbed back into the wagon while Philip handed the last box to the waiting sailor on the dock.

"That seems to be the last of it," Philip said, patting the horse's neck.

Will looked down at him. "Are ye sure ye dinna need anything else for the journey? The Lady Elizabet left quite a few belongings. I'm sure I could get her maid to retrieve a few more things."

"Nay. We dinna want to draw too much attention to ourselves. And we're already bringing more than they requested. Dinna forget, I'm going to have to find a way to transport all of this once we reach port."

Philip glanced around the bustling dock and then back at Will with unmistakable concern creasing his brow. William scowled.

"I'll be fine, Philip," he said. "I'm not the same green boy that I once was."

"I ken that well enough, lad. If I didna think ye could handle yerself, I'd not send ye back to be our eyes and ears in Ramsay's ranks. But just because I trust ye doesna mean I'm happy with sending ye to spy on the devil himself."

William bit his tongue and tried to keep his impatience from erupting. He'd been riding raids with Philip and John, their cousin, better known as the Highland Highwayman in these parts, for years. But now that John was an outlaw in exile with the Lady Elizabet, the highwayman's crew had disbanded. Most of the men had gone on to seek other employment, both legal and not so legal.

William had managed to secure a position with Ramsay, the man who was responsible for John's arrest and ultimate exile. And who had vowed revenge on the men he considered responsible for his own downfall. Will's position in Ramsay's ranks had already afforded them much needed information on Ramsay's plans. He had been quiet lately, but Will had no doubt the moment Ramsay discovered John and Elizabet's whereabouts, he'd attack. And Will needed to be in place to send warning to his kin. So, as much as he appreciated his cousin's concern, it exasperated him. They'd always seen Will as a young, impetuous bungler. He'd hoped what he'd managed to accomplish with Ramsay's men had gone a long way to erase that perception.

"I promise I'll be fine," William said, looking down at Philip with fond exasperation.

"Aye, ye will," Philip said with a smile. "I've trained ye well. And ye've done a grand job keeping us apprised of Ramsay's actions. But that doesna mean I willna worry. Are ye sure ye wouldna rather accompany me to Glenlyon? I could use yer help."

Will smiled at Philip's obvious play on his sense of loyalty, pleading for help he didn't need.

"Stop worrying so, Cousin," William said. "I ken where to find ye if I need ye. Ye're the one I'm worried about."

"And why is that?"

William smiled with a wicked twinkle in his eye. "Lady Alice doesna seem the type to give up so easily."

Philip snorted, though he glanced back at the road leading to the docks with a wary eye. "Aye. Lady Elizabet's adventures seem to have put the ridiculous notion in Lady Alice's head that running away with outlaws is the best way to escape an unwanted marriage."

"And telling her otherwise didna work so well, I take it, since ye've not stopped watching the roads for her since we arrived."

Philip shook his head. "I'd have better luck talking to the stone wall in the castle privy."

William laughed, though he, too, kept searching the road. "Perhaps yer words made a dent, after all. It doesna look as if the lady is coming."

"Canna say I'm surprised," Philip said with a half smile. "I've no doubt she tried. She seems a thick-heided goat, that one. But the lady was daft to think she'd be able to make it one day away from her pampered existence. Let alone navigate the road to Dover by herself. Still, we canna be too careful of Ramsay's men. He'd do anything to get to John and the Lady Elizabet. And he kens well enough how she felt about Lady Alice. I've no doubt she's been watched, which means there's a good chance he's seen my face, as well. Take care, laddie. Careful or no, we may have been spotted together by someone who'd report it."

"Dinna fash, Cousin. I'll be well."

A bell sounded on the ship, and a sailor hollered down the gangplank to him.

"You'd best board, sir, if you're coming!"

"On my way." Philip turned to look at Will one last time and gave his thigh a pat. "Godspeed to ye then, young William."

"And to you, Cousin."

Philip nodded and hurried up the gangplank just as the sailors pulled it aboard. He stood at the deck and waved goodbye to William as the boat pulled out to sea.

Will waved back, though his gaze darted around the crowds gathered on the docks. And lingered on one person in particular.

He frowned as he watched the young woman. She seemed nervous. She, too, watched the ship Philip had just boarded as it sailed out to sea, but she seemed more interested in what was going on around her. Her hands were knotted in her skirts tight enough he could see her white knuckles from where he sat, and her gaze darted about as though she were watching a cat playing with a mouse.

What was she up to? The state of her clothing suggested she came from a comfortable home. Not the wife of a sailor or dockworker then. And not someone who frequented the docks, judging by her nervousness. And she seemed overly concerned with both the ship that had just departed and those who were on the docks watching it. As if she were looking for someone.

Philip, maybe?

Tension settled in his gut, and he gritted his teeth. As far as he was aware, Ramsay didn't have anyone watching the ships for signs of the MacGregors. But that didn't mean he hadn't caught wind of Philip being in town. And if that were the case, he might have sent someone to follow him. Someone who might seem innocent, who would never be recognized as a spy.

Though if he'd wanted to send someone who would go

unnoticed, he should have chosen a different woman. The one slowly making her way up the docks was far too beautiful to blend into a crowd. Her auburn hair shone with tones of red and gold in the early morning sun, and she carried herself with a confident elegance that stood out in the crowd of ruffians on the dock, despite her nervousness.

He didn't know who she was, but it was obvious she didn't belong there. And he needed to find out why she was there. If she was a spy for Ramsay, one he didn't know about, then Will needed to make sure she didn't betray Philip's presence on that ship. Which meant he and his mystery woman needed to have a little chat.

Chapter Two

Rose stood at the docks, watching as the ship began to slowly pull away from shore. She couldn't believe she'd let her mistress talk her into this mad scheme. She'd been the personal maid of Lady Alice since their early teens, and her ladyship had always been headstrong and impulsive. But running away from her betrothed, with a savage Highlander whom she'd blackmailed into escorting her, was a piece of work, even for Lady Alice.

Rose glanced around the dock. As usual, it was a swarm of people. Sailors scurried about, loading and unloading other ships. Passengers, town folk, and other people milled about. Rose could only pray that there were no spies for the notorious Mr. Ramsay, the man who presented danger not only to Lady Alice, but to her dear friends as well. If Ramsay were to discover that Lady Alice was on that ship—and then discover her destination—many lives would be in danger.

Her eyes kept darting to and fro, trying to be sure no one watched the ship, or her, or...looked suspicious in general. A tall task, considering some of the characters on the docks.

Finally, once she was certain the ship was well underway, she turned to leave. It was best that she get back to the Chivers' inn before anyone noticed that Lady Alice was missing. She must keep her lady's whereabouts a secret for as long as possible. It was early enough they should be fine for a few more hours. But if anyone decided to open the lady's door before Rose was there to intercept them, all her carefully laid plans would be in jeopardy.

Before she got more than a few steps, a man she hadn't noticed stepped up to her side and grabbed her arm.

"What are you—?"

"Dinna make a sound," he said, drawing her close enough that she could feel the tip of his dagger pressing into her side under the cover of their cloaks.

"What do you want?" she whispered, trying to keep her wits about her, though her legs trembled so badly it was a wonder she remained upright.

"You and I are going to have a little chat," he said. "Let's go."

He led her off the docks. She didn't fight him, even with every muscle in her body tense and ready to do so. Causing a scene might save her, but it would most assuredly bring unwanted attention. No one could discover the Lady Alice was gone until it was too late for them to do anything, and the ship was still visible in the distance. Her lady needed more time to escape.

But when the man led her toward a wagon she dug in her heels. He kept his face in the shadow of his hat so she couldn't get a good look at him. His voice hadn't sounded familiar. But if he was someone who meant her no harm, he wouldn't have a dagger pressed to her ribs. If he was going to kill her, she'd rather he did it where her body might be found. And where he couldn't have a chance to prolong her suffering before ending her life.

Why had she ever left London? She should have tried harder to talk her mistress out of her mad scheme. A rush of homesickness for the nice, safe room in the Chivers' London townhouse overwhelmed her, and she wished, more than anything, that she was back home.

"I demand you release me at once," she said, taking care not to raise her voice loudly enough to draw attention.

"I'll do no such thing."

They'd reached the wagon, and she waited for her chance to flee. Hopefully, he'd put her in the bed of the wagon, which might afford her the opportunity to jump out and escape.

Either he had the same thought or simply wanted to keep her close, because instead of tossing her into the wagon bed, he grasped her arm tighter and all but shoved her up front onto the driver's bench. He was so close behind her she couldn't even throw herself over the other side. He sat, pulled her down beside him, and wrapped an arm about her shoulders.

"Take the reins," he said, tightening his grip on her shoulders and keeping the knife to her side.

She hesitated for only a second, but it was enough for him to press the blade in until she gasped from the sharp prick. She glared at him but gathered the reins. He nodded. "Good. Now take us onto the road. Stay to the side and dinna say a word."

"I thought you wanted to chat," she said through clenched teeth.

"Aye. Once we are away from prying eyes."

Her heart thundered at that. She had to get away before they got too far from town. Who knew what his plans would be once they were alone?

She kept an eye out for an opportunity. If she could escape without worrying about drawing attention to herself, she'd scream her fool head off and let the blackguard next to her do what he might. But with Lady Alice's scheme hanging in the balance… Rose sighed. And then sat up straighter. Up ahead of them was a bend. The road was lined with shrubbery, and a small copse of trees lay beyond it. There weren't too many travelers. If she could break away and make it to the trees before the man could follow, she might be able to hide in the woods. She'd have a minute or two headway as he'd have to deal with the horses before following.

She shifted in her seat, trying to put a few inches between them. He'd loosened his grip slightly, and his knife, while still poised and ready, no longer pressed into her side. The bend neared, and she tightened her grip on the reins. Just before it was upon them, she lifted her arms and brought the reins down with a *crack*, shouting "Yah!" to the horses.

The horses shot forward with a burst of speed, and the momentum flung Rose and the man back in their seats.

"What are ye doing?" he hollered.

He'd let go of her when he fell back, and she wasted no time. She grabbed hold of the sideboard and flung herself from the wagon. She landed on one of the blessed bushes which thankfully lessened the brunt of her fall. However, disentangling herself slowed her down. The man managed to bring the horses to a halt and shouted at her again. She didn't pause to listen.

She gathered her skirts and ran into the trees as fast as she could. His footsteps thundered behind her but she didn't stop. She did, however, look back over her shoulder once. He was much closer than she thought. She ran faster, turning around right as he shouted, "Wait!"

A blinding pain shot through her head as she collided with a low hanging branch. It knocked her off her feet, flat onto her back. The last thing she saw before the darkness closed in around her was the man standing over her, his arms reaching out.

· · ·

"Lass?" William reached out and brushed her hair from her face, his fingers gingerly pressing along her head as he checked for wounds. She seemed to be fine, albeit unconscious. And a stunning beauty even out cold on the forest floor. Too bad she was probably a spy for his worst enemy.

He held his hand in front of her face. She still breathed. And there was no blood, but she'd have a headache when she awoke for certain.

"Who are ye, lass? *Hmm?* Friend or foe?"

She didn't respond. He sighed and gathered her up, swinging her into his arms with a grunt. Thankfully, she hadn't made it too far.

"Ye're lucky, lass. If I had to trudge a greater distance with you in my arms, I might have left ye there."

He ignored the nagging voice in the back of his head that contradicted that lie. Yet, leaving her in the woods would accomplish his objective just as well as taking her prisoner. Mayhap more so, as taking her meant bringing her straight to the man for whom he suspected she worked.

"Leaving ye would make things a great deal easier," he said, realizing full well he was speaking to someone who couldn't speak back. Still, speaking aloud to her made her dead weight seem less heavy.

"I ken I dinna have much to go on yet, since ye went and skelped yerself in the head before I could question ye. But then, if ye dinna want to be taken for questioning, ye really should ha' acted less suspicious on the docks. Truly, the fact that ye were there at all…well, I kent it in my gut. And I mean to hear ye admit that ye're a spy for Ramsay. As ye most likely are. Why else would ye be standing there where ye have no business t'be, looking as suspicious as the day is long? Ye'd certainly been watching the ship that my kinsman was on, that much is certain."

He took a deep breath. "I dinna think ye'd made it so far into the woods, lassie. Good on ye. Except that now I have to haul ye back. Ye're no' but a wee thing, but still..." He hefted her up a bit higher with a groan. "It would help a fair bit if ye could wake and maybe put yer arms about my neck."

Instead, her head lolled against his shoulder. He glanced down at her peaceful features. "No? All right then, lass. If ye insist on being carried."

He walked a couple more feet before he started talking out loud again. "I ken ye'll no' likely thank me for taking ye from the docks. But I'll have ye ken, 'twas a fair risk for me to do so. I'm sure ye'll no' appreciate the courage it took. Understandable."

He laughed at his own joke and hefted her up again. "But I couldna leave ye free to report my kinsman's whereabouts to Ramsay. Although, I do find it unfortunate that my honor wouldna allow me to leave a defenseless woman in the woods, even if ye dinna prove innocent. Ye're a bonnie lass, but ye're breaking my back, if ye dinna mind me saying so."

He shifted her weight the best he could. If he could throw her over his shoulder, it would be much easier carrying her. But that would force all the blood into her head and give her an even more wicked headache than the one she'd already have. Best to suffer through the dead weight and be thankful he wouldn't have to carry her too much farther.

He glanced down at her again. "Still asleep, lassie?" He nodded. "Right then."

He took another deep breath and let it out with relief when he caught sight of the bush where he'd tied the horse and hidden the wagon. "Aye, saints be praised," he muttered.

Her weight felt a bit lighter now that the end was in sight. Or perhaps his arms had begun to go numb. Either way, he was thankful for the reprieve from his screaming muscles. He'd obviously been lying about too much while in Ramsay's employ. His cousins would never let him get away with such laziness. There were always chores to be done at the MacGregor households. He'd hated that as a child, but he had to admit, the constant activity had kept him strong and finely honed.

He made it to the wagon and laid her in the back. "Sorry, lass. I wasn't expecting passengers so, unfortunately, I have no straw. But," he said, balling up a handful of her cloak to cushion her head, "hopefully this will help a bit."

He patted her down, feeling through the material of her clothing looking for weapons. "Ye'll pardon me, I hope, but I canna be too cautious. I've spent too long infiltrating Ramsay's group and earning the blackguard's trust to let some woman ruin everything now. Ramsay wouldn't hesitate to run me through if he thought he'd been betrayed. And I'd lose any advantage my inside knowledge has given my kin, if I'm dead. With my position as one of Ramsay's men, I can keep an eye on things and report anything suspicious to my kinsman Philip, who in turn, reports to our other kinsmen John and Malcolm, the laird of the MacGregors, who everyone calls The Lion. Get all that, did ye? I hope so, because I'll no' repeat it."

A quiet snore escaped her lips, and William snorted. "Ah," he said in triumph, extracting a small but wicked looking dagger from her pocket. "I'll return this to ye if ye prove ye're no enemy to me and mine."

He bound her hands and feet, tight enough to keep her from escaping but loose enough they weren't too uncomfortable. He wasn't a monster for all that he felt like one when he gagged her with the clean handkerchief from his pocket.

"My apologies for all this, lass. But if ye decide to grace us with yer presence again before I can get ye hidden, we'll both be in danger. Philip, my cousin, the man I'm sure ye saw on the docks, is a known associate of Ramsay's sworn enemies. Also my kinsmen. Aren't I the lucky lad? Ramsay, damn his eyes, has spies everywhere. As ye probably ken well enough as ye are most likely one of them. So. I'm afraid there is no way that I can allow ye, no matter how bonnie ye may be, to pose a threat to my kin. Ye've seen Philip, I'm certain. On the docks boarding the ship. And ye've seen me. As ye ken well. It is very possible ye've seen us together and if ye have, well, that puts me in a bind, does it no'?"

He made sure everything was secure and that she wouldn't be able to sit up in the wagon. The last thing he needed was for a trussed up maid to jump from his wagon, again, at an inopportune moment.

"Had ye sat tight for a few more minutes, ye foolish lass, we could have had our chat and, on the off chance ye'd proven innocent, I'd have let ye go on yer way. Now, I'm forced to take ye with me. Perhaps 'tis for the best. This way, I can ensure ye do no harm. And if ye are'na who I ken ye to be...well, ye still willna be telling anyone about anything ye've seen. At least until I'm a fair distance away from ye."

He hopped back into the wagon and grabbed the reins. He needed to make haste to return to Ramsay's camp. He'd already been gone too long. What he'd do with the blasted woman when he got there he still didn't know.

Chapter Three

A fierce pounding gradually invaded Rose's dreams. The pressure behind her eyes throbbed until she could no longer keep them closed. Though opening them was the last thing she wanted to do. Until she remembered what she'd been doing before everything had gone black.

She sat up with a gasp and immediately regretted it. She brought her hands up to her head...her bound hands. A rising tide of panic threatened to overwhelm her, but she forced herself to breathe, slowly and evenly, and take stock of her situation.

Her hands were bound but she wasn't harmed or hampered in any other way. Her mouth was dry as toast and a bit sore at the edges. She wasn't currently gagged but, from the way she felt, she most likely had been. She lay on a cloak covering a pile of straw in what looked like the ruined remains of what might have once been a parlor or receiving room of an old manor house. The straw was clean, as was the rest of the space, despite the slightly musty smell that seemed to permeate old buildings. The room also sported a huge, ornate hearth that unfortunately did not contain a roaring fire. She shivered and shrank farther into her cloak. The man who'd taken her was nowhere to be seen.

She tried pulling her wrists apart, testing how tight the ropes were. There was a little leeway. Enough to keep the rope from cutting into her skin. Not enough for her to pull her hands free. Her feet were thankfully not bound, though a slight redness around her ankles suggested they had been. How long had she been asleep?

She brought her wrists to her lips and tugged at the rope with her teeth, inwardly cursing the tree she had run into. Of all the stupid mistakes to make. Next time, she'd take better care to watch where she was going.

"I'd be careful there, lass. That's a fine way to damage a perfectly good set of teeth."

The voice behind her made her jump, and she spun around to find the man who'd taken her standing in the doorway, holding a bowl of something steaming. She scrambled backward but there was nowhere to go but up against the wall.

"I'll no' hurt ye, lass."

"I'm afraid the evidence suggests otherwise."

His lips twitched and she narrowed her eyes at him, surprised that he seemed amused rather than angry at her insolence. Not very villainous of him. Nor was the handsome face that was half hidden in the shadows. She relaxed for a split second and then tensed her muscles again. Pleasant features did not mean he was harmless. Not all devils looked the part.

"My apologies, lass," he said. "Perhaps I should have said I have no intention of hurting ye further."

She scowled and held up her bound hands. "This is not hurting me? Kidnapping me and bringing me to this…this… *place* is not hurting me?"

He shrugged. "Aye, well it's no' my finest hour, I'll give ye that. But I meant what I said. Ye'll come to no further harm. And if ye dinna prove a threat, ye'll be free to go on yer way."

She snorted. "You expect me to believe you?"

He gave her a faint smile at that. "I probably wouldna if I were in yer position. But I swear on my mother's grave, I speak the truth."

She still didn't trust him, but her heart calmed some of its frantic beating at that.

"I brought ye something to eat," he said, nodding at the bowl. He set it close to her and stepped back.

Smart. She'd had every intention of bashing him in the face if he'd gotten close enough. The amused look in his eye told her he was very aware of that intention.

She eyed the bowl suspiciously.

"It's not poisoned," he said. "I canna get any information from ye if ye're dead."

Well, that was true enough. And if she was going to escape, she'd need her strength. She picked up the bowl and sniffed at the contents. Some sort of stew. She took a cautious sip. Not bad. Not great, but not bad. And it was warm and filling.

The man waited until she'd eaten her fill and then snagged the bowl from her before she had a chance to sling it at his head. He sat down on a stool near her and rested his elbows on his knees so he could stare right into her eyes. She wanted to lower her gaze, but she wouldn't show any sign of weakness. She straightened up and glared at him.

"Who are ye, then?" he asked. "And what were ye doing on the docks this morning?"

"I don't see how that is any of your business."

His faced hardened, and he leaned forward. "Dinna make this harder than it needs to be, lass. Answer the question."

She swallowed, not wanting to put herself in more danger.

But answering would put her mistress in danger. In fact, it was probably already too late. Without Rose there to cover for her, Lady Alice's absence was surely already known. Rose could only hope no one would guess she'd sailed away.

"Who are *you*, then? Why does a barbarian Scot," she said with a sneer, "have any interest in the identity of a simple maid?"

He ignored the insult, either because he was used to them or didn't have the sense to realize he'd been insulted. She assumed the latter. "A maid? For whom?"

Damn. She hadn't meant to betray any information. "It doesn't matter."

"Aye. It matters a great deal. Why were ye on the docks?"

She hesitated and then decided it couldn't hurt to reveal a little of the truth. Maybe it would be enough to placate him. "I was running an errand for my mistress."

"Yer mistress had an errand for ye? There? Seems like a more fitting job for one of the menfolk of the house."

Rose shrugged. "That's not for me to say. I do as I'm told."

"Somehow, I doubt that."

She glared at him again. "Doubt it all you want. You asked, I answered. Now let me go. My mistress will be frantic with worry. Wait...how long have I been here? And where is *here*?"

William raised an eyebrow and for a miserable second she didn't think he'd answer. Then he shrugged, "Ye dinna need to worry about where *here* is. As for how long, a few hours. Ye hit yer head—"

"A few hours?" She struggled against her bounds anew and tried to stand, panic rushing through her. "I have to leave. I must get back. If my mistress's family discover she's gone—"

She stopped short, belatedly realizing she'd revealed too much.

The man narrowed his eyes. "Who is yer mistress? And where has she gone?"

"Let me go," she said, shaking her bound hands at him. She wouldn't betray any more.

The man frowned, his eyes focusing on her as if he'd pull all her secrets out whether she willed it or no.

"Why were ye at the docks, lass? Did ye accompany yer mistress there?"

Rose stopped at that, chest heaving from her exertions. "I cannot say. Please let me go. Before it's too late." Her chin trembled, and she swallowed back the tears, angry that her frustration and anxiety had driven her to that point. She didn't want to give the wretch the satisfaction of seeing her cry.

The man seemed to hesitate before making some sort of decision. He leaned forward and spoke low and quiet. "Is yer mistress the Lady Alice? Was she meeting a man on the ship that sailed today?"

Rose gasped. "How did you know that?"

"Christ," he said, leaning back before banging his fist on his knee. He paced around the room before coming back to her.

When she saw the knife in his hand she shrank back against the wall.

He released a frustrated sigh. "I'm no' going to hurt ye, lass. Just cutting yer ropes."

She didn't trust that he told her the truth, but if he really wanted to hurt her, he could have done so many times over already. She held her hands out. But before he cut them, he leaned in again.

"I'll release ye and take ye back to town. But ye mustna make a sound and dinna try to run. Ye are surrounded by enemies here. If ye want to live and make it back home, ye're going to have to trust me and do as I say."

She raised an eyebrow at that and he at least had the grace to give her a slightly sheepish half grin. "Aye, I ken very well that trusting me willna be easy, but believe me when I say I'm the only thing that will keep ye safe here." He grabbed hold of the ropes binding her hands and leaned in farther. "Also believe me when I tell ye the last thing I want to do is draw attention to yer mistress and my kinsman."

She startled at that. *His kinsman?*

"But if ye try to escape me, that's exactly what ye'll be doing. Understand?"

Not even remotely. But she nodded anyway, desperate to get free of the ropes. She'd worry about whether or not to trust him later.

He watched her for half a heartbeat more and then quickly sliced through the ropes.

The second he looked down to slip his dagger back into its sheath, she jerked her still clenched hands up, clipping him right under the chin. He staggered back, one hand to his face, and she darted in the opposite direction as fast as she could.

She made it three steps before strong arms wrapped around her waist and hauled her back. He kept her pressed tight against him, one arm around her waist, the other across her shoulders like an iron band.

"Did I no' just say that running will only put ye in danger?"

"I'm sorry," she said, struggling against him. "Let me go and I promise I'll stay put this time."

He snorted and then froze as the sound of voices floated in from another room. He squeezed her harder and she stopped struggling. "Listen to me if ye want to live. I ken well ye have little cause to trust me, but I vow to ye I'm no danger to ye. That is not true of the men about to come in this door. They'll slit ye through with barely a bat of their eyes, if they dinna do worse to ye first. I'll explain all to ye, but for now, ye're going to have to stay put and trust me. Do ye understand?"

The terror bleeding into her veins made any movement difficult, but she forced a nod.

He turned her around so they faced each other, only inches apart. "Do as I say, without hesitation, and dinna speak a word unless I bid ye to, aye?"

She nodded again.

He glanced toward the door as the voices got louder and swore under his breath. "They are going to question yer presence here. I'll…tell them something to explain ye. But if anything happens to me, run as fast and far as ye can."

Her eyes widened, and he grasped her chin. "Do ye understand me, lass?"

She nodded again and then…he dragged her to him and kissed her, his lips claiming hers while his arms wrapped around her like a vise. She was too stunned to struggle and then it was too late, because the room was suddenly full of men. Who, after their initial surprise, were all staring at her as if they'd like to run her through with their swords. Or something more sinister. Suddenly, the man who held her, whose name she still didn't know, didn't seem quite so dangerous.

"Well, what do we have here?" one of them said, a cruel smile twisting his face.

Rose froze at her man's side, terror clawing at her. Her eyes darted around the room. There were at least ten men, all armed, all dangerous looking. And only one exit.

"William!" one of the men said. "You've returned. And brought with you a little surprise, eh? Well done, brother!"

Rose gasped. *Brother?*

May the saints preserve her. He was one of them.

• • •

William tore his lips from the maid and plastered what he hoped was a properly leering smile on his face. He turned to face the men, keeping the woman as far behind him as he could. Not that he felt any safer standing in front of her. If she had any knives on her, other than the one he'd found in her pocket, he had no doubt she wouldn't hesitate to shove it between his ribs. He could even admit he deserved it. But it would be best if she didn't do so yet.

"So, who do we have here?" Lionel asked.

William pushed her a little farther behind him, and thankfully she didn't protest. "She's nobody to concern yourself with."

"Well that's easier said than done when you bring her here," Lionel said. "Mr. Ramsay doesn't like strangers. And bringing her around this lot might not have been the wisest course of action."

William nodded. "Well, as ye can see, she's no' exactly a stranger to me," he said, giving the man a playful wink. "And I didna have much choice. The lass follows me wherever I go."

Several of them laughed and nudged each other, and Lionel's expression lost a little of his suspicion. But he still wasn't going to let it go. "Mr. Ramsay won't be happy to find her here."

William nodded again. "I ken that well enough, but the poor lass is miserable without me. I'm afraid she may do herself harm if she's left all alone. Best if I have her where I can keep an eye on her. I promise ye, she willna be any trouble."

"Well I don't know about that, mate," one of the other men said, stepping forward. "Seems like she might be too much for you to handle. I'd be more than happy to help out if you find you've got your hands full."

The other men laughed, and William kept a tight rein on the sudden flash of rage that surged in him at the thought of anyone else touching her. "That's all right, friend," he said. "I can manage my woman on my own."

"Oh, your woman, is she?" Lionel asked. "I didn't hear her opinion on the matter. Maybe you have to keep such a close eye on her because if you didn't, she'd run off."

That hit a little too close to home, but William stood his ground.

"Enough of this," Lionel said. "Keep her quiet and out of sight. Mr. Ramsay should be back in a few hours, and the last thing you want is to provoke him."

William nodded again but didn't move from his protective stance until the rest of the men had cleared out. Only then did he relax, not realizing how ready for a fight he had been until the tension drained from his muscles. He let out a deep breath and turned around. The woman might be a thorn in his side but at least she knew when to keep quiet.

He nodded at her. "It looks like ye have some brains about ye after all."

She scowled. "I might be angry enough to run you through, and I'll certainly never forgive you for what you've done, dragging me into a den of murderous brigands, not to mention the mess you've made of everything. But that doesn't mean I'm stupid. If you had wanted to kill me you could've done so when I was unconscious or when we were back in the woods. There's no point in you dragging me all the way here just to kill me in front of all these witnesses. So whatever your plans for me, I figured they must be better than what that lot had in mind."

William snorted. "Accurate assumption."

"So...what *are* you planning to do with me?" she asked.

William sighed and sat on a stool and motioned for her to do the same. She looked as if she'd protest again but instead she slumped back into a chair and stared at him, waiting.

"I think there might have been a misunderstanding

here," he said.

She raised an eyebrow at him. "And what misunderstanding would that be?"

"What is yer name? And dinna waste time with lying or hesitating."

She looked as if she wouldn't answer him and then with an exasperated sigh she said, "Rose Thatcher."

"And yer mistress?"

Her face twisted like she'd rather chew glass then answer him but she finally said, "Lady Alice Chivers."

At that name William closed his eyes and rubbed his hands over his face. "And would yer mistress have been meeting a Mr. Philip McGregor on the boat that sailed from Dover this morning?"

Rose sat up straight at that, her eyes going wide. "How did you know that?"

He sighed again and shook his head. What an absolute, bloody nightmare. "Because Philip McGregor is my kinsman. My cousin. We didna think yer lady would meet him, since we didna see her when we arrived. Then, when I saw ye on the dock looking suspiciously out of place, watching the ship, the only conclusion I could come to was that ye were spying for Mr. Ramsay."

She raised another eyebrow at that. "That's the *only* conclusion you could draw? That I was a spy? For the same Mr. Ramsay that you apparently work for?"

"I didna say it was a good assumption," he said, more sheepishly than he would have cared to let on. "And my being here with Ramsay…it's not what ye think. I canna explain it now." His eyes glanced at the door through which the other men had left. "But let me assure ye my motives are in line with yers."

"Then you must let me go," Rose said, leaning forward to raise pleading eyes to his. "I was supposed to return back to the inn where my mistress's family is staying. Her plan was for me to inform the others that she was ill and keep anyone from noticing she was not there for as long as possible. But if I have already been gone for several hours I fear her absence may have been discovered. If that is the case..."

Dread settled in William's gut. "If that is the case, then the entire town will be on the lookout for yer mistress," he said, swallowing hard. "And my kinsman."

Rose nodded and sat back with a frustrated snarl. "All you had to do was tell me who you were and this all could have been sorted out on the docks. If I had known you were a friend to the man my mistress sailed with, instead of an enemy, I would have told you all. Instead you jumped to conclusions, kidnapped me, and now my mistress and your cousin are both in danger."

"Not to mention those they are protecting," William added, rubbing his hand over his face. "Aye, lass, I'm well aware how terrible a mistake this is."

Rose frowned at that, confusion furrowing her brow, but before she could say much else someone shouted William's name. He scowled and then stood and brushed his legs off. "I'll try to spirit ye away later tonight, but I must go take care of a few things. Dinna leave this room or speak to anyone. If anyone comes near ye..."

He frowned, pressing his lips together as he weighed the pros and cons of arming her. Finally, he released an exasperated sigh and pulled her dagger from his waistband, pressing it into her hand.

"Where did you get this?" she asked, her eyes widening with surprise. And anger. Not surprising considering he stole it from her.

"I took it off ye when ye were unconscious. It didna seem a prudent choice to leave ye armed."

Her lips twitched. She might have laughed if he hadn't

been about to abandon her to a room full of mercenaries. His gut twisted at the thought. "If anyone but me comes near ye, dinna hesitate to use that. I'll try not to be too long."

She held the dagger up and took a step closer to him, pointing it at his throat. He didn't truly believe she'd use it, despite the anger still burning in her eyes. But his heart still thudded uncomfortably in his chest.

"And what if I choose to use it on you?" she asked.

He shrugged, forcing a nonchalance he didn't feel. "Ye can if ye'd like, but then who would save ye from them?" He jerked his head over his shoulder in the direction of the other men.

She hesitated for a second. They both knew he had a point. With him she could be relatively sure she would come to no harm. With the others... He doubted she had any desire to chance it. She might be able to defend herself against one man, but not so many. She gave him a sharp nod and took a step back.

He didn't truly think she'd be in danger or he wouldn't leave her. The men in Ramsay's gang were criminals, but reasonably well controlled. And he wouldn't be far. Still, he hesitated to leave her until his name was shouted once more. Then he spun on his heels. "I'll be back as soon as I can," he said.

"And what exactly am I supposed to do while you're gone?" she asked.

He paused. "They think ye're my woman. Do womanly things."

She rolled her eyes and he left the room chuckling. The woman might be a thorn in his side, but she was a beautiful one. Strong, brave, and intelligent as well. Not traits he typically looked for in a woman. When he sought a woman out it was for temporary companionship. He'd never had a desire to spend more than a few pleasant hours with any of the women he'd known previously.

This one, however...with those flashing eyes and the way her cheeks flushed slightly when she had her dander up. Those full lips that he wanted to kiss even as they berated him. And there was a sharp wit behind that pretty face, one he wanted to explore.

If she could get over her desire to kill him for his admittedly stupid mistake, they might actually get along.

Might being the operative word.

Chapter Four

Rose watched him walk away, taking in every inch of his physique. She'd already noted his height; he actually had to duck beneath the doorway. Her nose barely reached his throat, and she'd had to crane her neck when standing beside him. His long legs were encased in breeches rather than the kilt she'd always assumed his people favored. Must be because he was in England instead of his native land. And in her more civilized country, men didn't go about wrapped up in lengths of fabric. So, of course, he'd need to dress properly to fit in. Except that deep voice touched with his Scottish brogue betrayed him the moment he spoke. Some women would probably find such a rich-toned voice to be alluring, but not her. She'd barely been affected at all. Any flutterings she felt were due entirely to her dire situation.

She bit her lip and paced around the room, trying to make sense of everything. Could she really trust William? He had been the one to kidnap her, after all. Yet…he seemed genuinely upset at his actions. In fact, as he'd walked away, his broad shoulders had appeared slightly hunched. Maybe from the weight of their plight. From guilt? He had apologized. Admitted his mistake. That was a great deal more than most men would do. He'd looked so distraught she almost felt sorry for him. Almost.

He somehow managed to inspire both sympathy and sheer fury in her. It was a curious sensation. She'd never wanted to simultaneously comfort and maim a man before. Leave it to a Scot. Was it all Scots or only the MacGregors who were prone to wreak havoc on innocent lives? She'd never met a Scot who wasn't a MacGregor, so she couldn't be sure. The one thing she was certain about—the MacGregors were trouble.

First, Philip had gone and seduced her mistress into some harebrained scheme, because no matter what Lady Alice said about blackmailing the man, there was no missing the lovesick glint in her eye when she'd spoken of him. This, of course, after Laird John MacGregor, who was a notorious highwayman, no less, had seduced Lady Alice's bosom friend into running off with him, putting the idea in Alice's head in the first place.

Then, when Rose had been doing nothing but minding her own business, William had up and kidnapped her, without even bothering to make sure he had cause. And despite this mess being entirely his fault, she still had to smother the urge to comfort *him*. The nerve!

She sighed. Maybe it was the eyes. Lady Alice had talked about Philip's. How his deep blue eyes seemed to sear right into a lady's soul. Perhaps it was a family trait, because every time Rose looked into William's, her stomach tossed about like the time she'd taken a tumble down the kitchen stairs. As if she was about to scream or be sick, yet still felt so alive and…exhilarated, all at once.

She frowned, trying to restoke her anger. She'd need to steel herself against such thoughts. He was the reason she was in danger. The reason Lady Alice was in danger. She needed to quash any soft urges to reach out and take his hand to offer some support. Or any other urges he might inspire. Because he deserved nothing of the sort from her. What he deserved was a good tongue lashing.

She put her hands on her hips and took stock of her surroundings, resolved to put William from her mind. The building had probably been a beautiful manor once and could be again, with a little care…and a full ceiling. She looked up at the gaping hole in one corner and pulled her cloak more tightly about her. The room did offer shelter from most of the elements, and for that she was grateful. But she couldn't stop worrying about what was going on back in town.

Her mistress had been very explicit in her instructions. Rose was to have gone straight back to their lodgings and camped in front of her door. If anyone came looking for her, Rose was to inform them her mistress was ill. But with no one there to keep them from opening the door, it was only a matter of time before her mistress's disappearance was discovered. If it hadn't been already. Since Lady Alice had been in a fine temper over her impending betrothal and had made no secret of the fact that she wanted to see no one, it was possible her family had decided to leave her be. She hoped.

Rose's disappearance, on the other hand, would cause greater upset, at least in the servants' quarters. When her mistress had no need of her, Rose helped the other maids or serviced the other ladies in the family. With the family preparing for a long journey, Rose would certainly have been needed. If they had to go search for Rose, the first place they would look would be her mistress's quarters. Which made the probability that their absence had been discovered, nearly certain.

Rose paced back and forth across the room, her impatience and anger growing with every step. That stupid man! If he had let her alone, everything would have turned out fine. How could he think that she was a spy? Did she really look so sinister? All she'd been doing was standing on the dock, watching the ship. Not skulking around warehouses or whispering with nefarious looking sailors.

The man was insufferable! Intense, soulful eyes and deep, rumbly voice aside. There was obviously nothing behind his abnormally handsome face than gruel for brains.

What kind of man, rather than simply introduce himself, felt the best course of action was to kidnap a total stranger? He was daft, that was the only explanation. She would never forgive him for this. Never. He'd ruined everything.

She tightened her grip on the dagger now safely back in her skirt pocket—after he'd stolen it! Thief!—while daydreams of what she would like to do to him flitted through her head. She ignored the fact that his chiseled features and broad shoulders would have led to much different daydreams in other circumstances. He must be very strong to have carried her all the way from the woods. She had gone quite a ways in.

She snorted, mentally berating herself. What sort of fool was she, mooning over how strong he must have been *when he carried her unconscious body* to his wagon so he could abduct her? He deserved a good lashing. Or worse.

Except, she couldn't kill him yet. She needed him to get her out of the situation he'd gotten her in. Not that she would actually be able to kill him. But it was a fun idea.

When she finally grew tired of pacing, she sat on the stool he had vacated and glanced around the room again. Exactly what womanly tasks there were to do escaped her. There didn't seem to be much in the room. It was pretty bare, consisting only of two stools and a makeshift bed in the corner, made of a pile of straw and some blankets. And a rickety table by the door. There was a basket on the table that, upon closer inspection, had some knitting that was in the process of being done. A new pair of socks. For William?

The notion of helping him out in any way did not sit well with her but neither did sitting there doing absolutely nothing. She would go mad if she had to stay in there without anything to occupy her except her own thoughts.

With a long-suffering sigh, she took the basket back to the stool and pulled out the darning needles. She began to work, the clicking of the needles a comforting sound in the silence of the room. More time than she realized had passed before she heard footsteps in the hallway. The darkening sky that showed through the hole in the ceiling told her evening had arrived.

The pit of anxiety in her stomach grew larger. Surely her absence, and most likely her mistress's, had been discovered by now. The household would be in an uproar. She could only hope her mistress had had enough of a head start to get cleanly away and that no one had noticed her getting on the ship who could tell her parents where she had gone.

If only William hadn't taken her!

She gripped the knitting needle in her hand tightly, and when he entered the room she stood ready to give him another earful of her anger.

Only it wasn't William.

One of the other men who had been in the group earlier leaned against the doorframe, leering at her suggestively. He licked his lips, looking her up and down. She tried to repress the shiver that ran down her spine but obviously wasn't successful. His low, sinister chuckle reverberated through her, leaving fear in its wake.

"Now, there, girlie, you don't need that," he said, glancing at the needle in her hand. "There's no need to be afraid of me," he said. "I think we'll get along fine."

"Do you now?" she asked, forcing the words out, proud she could do so without her voice shaking.

"I don't see why not. If you're friendly to me, I'll have no reason not to be friendly in return."

She gripped the needles tighter and was somewhat comforted by the weight of the dagger in her pocket. He stepped farther into the room, and she looked over his shoulder hoping that William was behind him. But there was no one there.

"Come on now," he said. "It's been a good long while since I've had the company of a pretty maid such as yourself."

"Really?" she said. "I can't imagine why."

He shrugged his shoulders. "Not much time or opportunity to meet such a fine woman."

She would have thought that he was trying to sweet-talk her except the predatory look in his eyes said he didn't really care about her opinion of him or his suggestion.

"I'm sorry I can't be...friendlier. But I'm William's woman. I save my friendliness for him."

"Is that so?" he said, stepping closer.

She managed a nod.

"Well, then he should be here to guard you, don't you think?"

"He'll be back soon. I don't think he'll be pleased to find you in here."

"Unfortunately, young William is rather busy. It will probably be hours before he returns."

She tried backing up more but the cold stone of the wall pressed against her back. He grinned again, an expression that sent a shard of ice-cold terror into her gut. She started easing sideways, hoping she could break away at some point and rush across the room. But he followed her movements slowly, like he was trying to keep from spooking a deer.

"I'd hate for you to be lonely here all on your own. Why don't we get to know each other a little better? I'd be happy to keep you company until William returns."

"That's very kind of you," she said, not bothering to keep her tone friendly anymore, no matter what she said. "But no thank you. I am quite content to wait for him."

"No matter," he said. He half turned like he was going to leave but Rose didn't drop her vigilance. A lucky thing for her because in the next second, he twisted and lunged toward her. She jabbed out with the knitting needle, gouging him in the hand that reached for her. He howled in pain and swung with his other arm, catching her on the cheek. She dropped to her knees with a cry, her head ringing while black spots danced in her vision. She brought her hand up to her throbbing face, keeping the man in her sights despite the overwhelming desire to crumple to the ground. She couldn't withstand many more blows like that.

She fumbled in her pocket for the dagger and drew it, holding it in a trembling hand in front of her. The man laughed cruelly.

"And what are you going to do with that, little girl?" he asked.

"She's going to run ye through with it," William said. "And if *she* doesna, I will."

Rose sagged in relief, though she kept her dagger pointed at the man. He spun toward William, who radiated anger in the doorway.

"William. Good of you to join us. You know, you should take better care of your toys, or they're liable to get stolen. Or broken."

William shook his head, circling the man until he was able to put his body between him and Rose.

"Ye were told she was mine," William said. "That is the only warning ye should have required. But ye seem to have need of another."

The man shrugged. "If you cared for the woman you shouldn't have brought her here."

Before William could say anything else, the other man launched himself at him. William was ready for it and neatly dodged the blow, spinning so quickly he was able to land a fist right across the man's jaw.

More men filtered into the room, drawn by the scuffle. The man lunged again and Rose screamed a warning. William spun easily and grabbed the man from behind, wrapping an arm around his neck and pinning one arm behind his back. The man struggled, his legs kicking out as William slowly choked him.

Before anything else could happen, another man strode in. The furor died down and all the men backed against the wall, waiting. Rose's stomach coiled and twisted, her nerves fraying on a wave of apprehension as she took in the man all the others seemed to fear. This must be the notorious Mr. Ramsay. He looked around the group with cold, piercing eyes. His features were actually handsome and, if one didn't look too closely, he would be attractive. But the expression in his cold, dead eyes counteracted any beauty that could be found in his face.

"What is going on here?" he asked.

The man clutching at William's arm tried to respond but nothing came out, save for a strangled squawk. Ramsay looked at William. "Release him, Butler."

William dropped the man, pushing him so he landed on his knees in front of Ramsay. Rose frowned, glancing at him. Butler must be his alias for the group. Or was MacGregor the lie?

The man on the floor turned as if he would launch himself at William again, but a barked command from Ramsay held him still.

"What is going on here?" Ramsay asked again, looking at William.

"He attacked my woman," William said.

"The little bitch stabbed me," the man said, holding out his bleeding hand.

Ramsay snorted. "If you were foolish enough to tangle with a wildcat you're liable to get wounded." He glanced behind William, as if noticing Rose for the first time. He took her in, still crouched with a dagger and probably looking like a wildling, waiting to stab anyone who came near. His eyes held a hint of admiration, but she still shrank back under his scrutiny. He was the last man whose attention she wanted to draw.

"She is mine," William said. "And I defend what is mine."

Ramsay glowered at him and glanced at Rose.

He regarded her for a second and then his lips turned up in a smile that sent ice cascading through her veins.

"Let's see, shall we?"

"My lord?" William said. His face creased in a worried frown before he stepped in front of her again.

Ramsay glanced at them. "You say she is yours. Roger here wants her," he said, jerking his head at the other man. "We haven't had any entertainment in a few days. So." He drew a dagger and tossed it on the floor between the two men. "Let's see which one of you truly desires her. Winner claims her."

Rose's jaw dropped and William held his arm out to keep her behind him, only to shove her back toward the wall when Roger lunged for the dagger.

William drew his own blade and Rose slapped her dagger into his hand. She hated to give it up, but he couldn't lose, and a blade in each hand could mean the difference. She might not totally trust him, but she trusted him much more than the odious Roger. If her dagger would help William win, he was welcome to it.

The men circled each other. Roger slashed out a couple times, but William easily dodged him. Rose was beginning to think nothing more would happen when Roger lunged out and tackled William, knocking him to his back. They grappled on the floor, and Rose pressed her hands to her mouth to keep from shouting. She didn't want to distract William. Or draw attention to herself. The other men in the room were busy cheering on the fight. The last thing she wanted to do was remind anyone that no one was currently protecting her.

She wouldn't have to remind one man. A shiver ran down her spine, and she glanced up to find Ramsay's eyes fixed on her, his lips twisted in a cruel smile. He pinned her with that evil gaze for a few more moments before turning his attention back to the fight. She didn't have to wonder who he wanted to win, even before he shouted encouragement to Roger. She and William had stated they belonged to each other, and so Ramsay wanted to tear them apart. For no other reason than to cause pain, it seemed.

She sent up a silent prayer to bolster William and kept her back to the wall.

William had managed to flip Roger off him and reverse their positions so he was on top. It gave him enough leverage to get a few good punches in before Roger could fend them off. William had lost one of his daggers at some point. The remaining one was clutched in one hand while the other hand held back Roger's dagger from skewering him.

They each strained to reach the other. And then William reared back his head and slammed it forward, cracking it off Roger's head with a sickening crunch. The force of the blow smashed Roger's head against the floor.

He didn't lose consciousness, but it was enough for him to go limp.

William stood and shook his head, his chest heaving. Rose hurried to his side, propping herself under his arm to give him support. He held her close though he didn't lean on her. Whether he needed her support or not, she was grateful to have him by her side again, so she wrapped her arm about his waist and held tight.

Ramsay grimaced but nodded at William. "I guess you get to keep her after all."

William's jaw visibly clenched, but he merely nodded.

Ramsay jerked his head toward Roger. "Finish him."

William frowned again. "I believe he's learned his lesson, sir."

Ramsay glowered at William, his lip curling with disgust. "The only lesson here is that you're nothing but Scottish scum who can't follow orders."

William gripped Rose's shoulders to the point of pain, but she didn't make a sound.

"I simply dinna wish to deprive ye of one of yer men," William said, his voice strained with barely controlled anger.

Rose held her breath, waiting to see if Ramsay would call him out for it. But Ramsay merely sneered.

"You assume I want a man who can't hold his own in a fight for more than two minutes. I do not."

"My lord," Roger said, pushing himself up and holding out his hand.

He didn't get anything else out. Ramsay drew his sword and ran him through.

Rose slapped a hand to her mouth to keep her scream in, but she couldn't tear her eyes from the dead man lying in a pool of his own blood. William pulled her closer and slightly behind him, using his body to both shield her from the other men in the room and block Roger from her sight.

"Clean that up," Ramsay said to a few of the men. They hurried to do his bidding, dragging the body from the room. "Is there anyone else who wishes to challenge Butler for the woman?"

No one took him up on the offer and Rose sagged against William.

"Good," Ramsay said. "Now get out. You all have your tasks to do. We leave tomorrow. My little rabbit has finally left her den."

The grin that broke out on his face sent another chill down Rose's spine. William kept his attention on the other men but held his hand out behind him so she could grasp it. She didn't hesitate. She might not trust him but if she had to choose between him or the other men, she'd throw her lot in with William. A haggard-looking woman came in with a bucket and hastily scrubbed the blood from the floor. The fact that she didn't look horrified or surprised at her grim task filled Rose with apprehension. What sort of life must she live in this camp if cleaning up pools of blood had no effect on her?

After the room cleared, Ramsay turned to look at William and Rose. "Keep her under control if she will be traveling with us."

William nodded, and Ramsay looked her over again. "I suppose having another woman along on our journey could be useful. Maybe she can cook better than the hags currently preparing my food. Put her in charge of my meals, Butler. She can remain with you but don't let her interfere with your other duties."

William nodded again. "Thank you, my lord."

Ramsay left without another word. Some of the tension left William once the room was clear. He retrieved her dagger from where he'd dropped it and then turned back to her, looking her over.

"Are ye all right?" he asked. He gently brushed a thumb over her cheek. "Are ye hurt?"

She shook her head. "He hit me but I stabbed him before he was able to do anything else."

William smiled at her. "Ye're a brave lass, I'll give ye that. But I think while we're alone together," he wagged her dagger in the air, "I'll hold onto this."

She scowled at him. "You still don't trust me?"

He shook his head, his smile growing larger. "Not as far as I could throw ye, lass."

"Well the sentiment is returned, I assure you," she said.

He laughed at that.

"What was Ramsay talking about?" she asked. "Why are we leaving tomorrow? Who is the rabbit?"

William sighed, all amusement draining from his face. "Sit down. We have much to discuss."

Chapter Five

William debated how much to share with Rose but decided he might as well tell her all. She was in this with him now, like it or not.

"I dinna ken what yer lady told ye, but he is the one who is putting us all in danger, yer lady and my kinsmen, most of all. And he's just discovered yer lady is gone. We are all in danger now."

The color faded from Rose's face, and William frowned. "Are ye all right, lass?"

"Yes. I need a moment. I think…after everything…" She gestured to the door, and William realized it may have only now hit her how close she had come to real harm.

He reached for her slowly, gauging her reaction. She didn't object when he wrapped an arm around her shoulders, so he drew her in to his side and held her trembling form, trying to calm her.

"Ye did well," he said. "I'm actually quite impressed with ye. All things considered."

She managed to snort at that. "Because I am a woman?"

He shrugged. "Ye wouldna be the first woman I'd seen do well in a fight. Ye should see the lady of Glenlyon, Lady Sorcha, when she's in a dander. Or even Lady Elizabet, yer mistress's friend. When my laird first met her, she lunged out of a carriage and held a dagger to his throat," he said with a chuckle.

Her lips twitched at that, but the amusement faded quickly. "Then why do you sound like you don't approve of my actions?"

"I didna realize I did. Perhaps I'm merely angry at myself for putting ye in a position where ye needed to defend yerself."

"That makes two of us."

He laughed. "Here, I brought ye something to eat." He went back to the door and picked up a steaming bowl of stew and a lump of bread from the corner where he'd left them. "I'm sorry I canna offer ye more luxurious accommodations. We'll have to share my quarters, such as they are."

He gestured at the pallet made up in the corner, and she glanced up at him like her stomach was twisting on the bread that she had just swallowed.

"Dinna look at me like that, lass," he said with a tired note in his voice. "I have no designs on your virtue."

"Why not?" As soon as the words left her lips her eyes widened, her mouth a little *O* of either confusion or amusement, or maybe both. He cocked an eyebrow, and she blushed.

"I didn't mean...that is, I only meant..." His lips twitched and she sighed. "I simply meant that seems to be what all the other men are thinking so..."

"So why am I no' thinking the same?" he asked. She nodded, and he gave her a small smile. "Believe me, lass. Ye're bonnie enough for any man to want ye." His gaze roved over her. "But I prefer my lassies to be a bit more...docile."

She cocked her head at that, and he pointed to the dagger

she gripped in one hand. "Oh," she said with a slight laugh. "Sorry." She slipped it back in her pocket.

"Clever little pickpocket, are ye no'?"

She shrugged. "Not especially. I simply drew it from your belt when you turned to get the food."

He snorted. He'd have to keep a closer eye on her. "Now then," he said, "we have other things to concern ourselves with."

She hastily chewed the bite of stew in her mouth and put the bowl down.

He shook his head. "Finish that up, lass. We can talk while ye eat."

He sat beside her with his own bowl and chewed thoughtfully.

"Have you heard any news from town?" she asked.

"Aye," he nodded. "Yer mistress's disappearance has unfortunately been discovered, as has yer own. The Chivers family have the entire town out searching. They're questioning everybody, including those at the dock."

Rose put down the bowl, her face pale once more. "You must take me back. Perhaps I can help. I can tell them..."

"Aye? Tell them what?" Rose frowned and William nodded. "There's nothing ye can say that will make it any better. They'll only question ye and whether ye answer or no, ye'll be in a world of trouble. Not to mention, Ramsay now expects ye to be personally handling his meals. He didna question yer presence too closely, but if ye were to suddenly disappear, that would raise his suspicions. Like it or no, we are stuck together for now, lass."

Rose looked as if she'd argue, but then her shoulders slumped in defeat. "Will my lady and your kinsman be discovered?"

William frowned at that. "So far, no. I dinna think anyone saw your lady board the ship or if anyone had, he has not yet been discovered. It could take several days before they determine where she's gone."

Rose relaxed a little, and he hated to ruin that, but she needed to know everything. "However," he said, and she tensed again. "Witness or no, there are only so many places she could've gone. Either she took a horse and traveled by land or she boarded one of the ships. And the only ship that left the harbor today was the one she and my cousin were on. If her family is smart they will send runners in all directions, including to the next port where the ship will dock. If we are lucky, it will take them a day or two to think of that. At the very least, that will give them an entire day's sailing and they will likely reach their destination before any messengers can reach the ship."

"And if they are discovered?"

William put down his bowl. "There isna anything we can do about that. My cousin, Philip, will handle any issues that might arise. Although, from what I understand, he wasna too keen on escorting Lady Alice to Scotland."

Rose wouldn't meet his gaze, but she smiled at that. "The Lady Alice can be very...persuasive when she wants something."

"Persuasive, is it? It sounded a lot more like blackmail to me."

Rose opened her mouth to defend her mistress, but William held up a hand. "Arguing about Lady Alice and Philip's arrangement is pointless. That is between them and there's nothing we can do about it. We have more pressing concerns."

"Such as?" Rose asked.

"Ramsay has been watching yer lady's house since her friend, the Lady Elizabet, ran off with my kinsmen John."

"Why would he be doing that?" Rose asked, a confused furrow creasing her brow.

"It's a very long story," William said. "Ramsay is hell-bent on finding John and Elizabet. Knowing how close the ladies were, he knew there was a chance that watching Lady Alice would eventually lead him to Elizabet and John."

Rose sucked in a deep breath and let it out slowly. "And that's exactly what has happened, isn't it?"

"It's possible," William said, "though it may not be Lady Alice's actions alone that are at fault. Philip risked going to her in order to deliver a letter from the Lady Elizabet. I warned him against it, because Ramsay and his men would recognize Philip by sight. If he were seen at Lady Alice's home, they would have been alerted to his presence. That has made them extra vigilant in watching her. Ramsay has had a man in position there since I've been with his crew."

"And now that Lady Alice has disappeared?" Rose asked. By the look on her face, she already knew the answer.

William nodded. "Ramsay finally has the clue he has been after."

She took a deep breath and released it slowly, her face bleak. "So, what happens now?"

William sighed and sat back, rubbing his face. "Ramsay has been gathering men to march on Glenlyon. But until now, he hasna been in much hurry. I believe he wants to be sure he is better prepared this time."

"This time? Part of the long story you mentioned?"

William nodded. "Ramsay attacked Glenlyon once before. It didna end well for him, even with the full strength of the Campbell clan behind him. Or, most of the Campbells, anyway."

"The Campbells?"

William nodded again. "Ramsay isna his real name. He is the son of the Campbell chieftain. Ramsay tried to overthrow his father and persuaded a good number of his father's men into following him. He led an attack on Glenlyon that his father had to come help fight. Still, he had the support of many of his clansmen. Luckily our laird, Malcolm—"

Rose's eyes widened. "The one they call The Lion?"

"Aye."

"Even I've heard of The Lion," she said, awe in her voice.

William gave her a sharp nod. "He and the MacGregors were able to defeat Ramsay. His father had him exiled from the clan and sent to London. He should ha' been imprisoned, but Ramsay was able to use his mother's wealth and connections to buy his way out of trouble. He began calling himself by his mother's name—Ramsay. To distance himself from the Campbell clan. But he never forgot his humiliating defeat and has been determined to exact revenge on the MacGregors."

"How was all this kept quiet? I didn't hear a word of it. And servants hear everything," she said with a wry smile.

"I dinna think the elite of London care so much about what occurs in the Highlands of Scotland, lass."

She flushed a bit at that, but William carried on. "Matters were made worse when my kinsman John managed to destroy Ramsay's smuggling operation. John was a highwayman and, despite Ramsay revealing his identity, John was merely exiled instead of executed, as Ramsay had hoped. But when John left, he took the Lady Elizabet with him. She had been promised to Ramsay."

"So Ramsay has many reasons to hate the MacGregors," Rose said.

William laughed but there was no amusement in the sound. "Aye, many reasons," he agreed. "He has been waiting for the opportunity to exact his revenge. But he didna ken where John would be. John was exiled and has been traveling, but Ramsay kent that he would eventually return to Scotland. He's not supposed to return there, but as long as he stays out of England, the king will leave him be."

"But if Ramsay was defeated at Glenlyon once before, why would he think to attack it again?"

"We dinna think he will. Glenlyon is too well protected, which is why we think he's kept watch on those who were close to John who remained in England. In the hopes someone will lead him to John outside of Glenlyon."

"And those his lady was close to, like my Lady Alice?"

William nodded. "Exactly."

Rose paled, and William looked grim. "So now what do we do?" Rose asked. "We need to alert them."

"Agreed," William said. "That has been my purpose all along. I've been with Ramsay's group for many months now so that I could warn my kinsmen if he made a move."

"Then why are we still here? We need to go."

But William shook his head. "I'll send a messenger to Glenlyon tonight so they are aware of what has occurred and that Ramsay is likely headed their way. But I canna leave myself. We still dinna ken what exactly Ramsay is planning. He will travel to Glenlyon, certainly, but how many men will he have? When is he planning to attack? How is he planning to attack? Until I have more details, Glenlyon is better served if I remain at my post."

Rose frowned. "So we are just going to stay here?" she asked.

"For now. It doesna sit well with me either, lass," he said before she could complain again. "I'd like nothing more than to return home and leave the stink of this country behind me."

Rose glared at that but he ignored her. "For now, we will watch and wait and when we have more information, we will make our move. Besides, if I were to disappear now, it would only make Ramsay suspicious."

Rose scoffed and William frowned. "Dinna underestimate his intelligence. He would ken that there had been a spy in his midst and he would change his plans. No. We need to wait until we are closer to Glenlyon. Hopefully, we'll be able to slip away while his preparations are underway. When we better ken what they are. In the meantime, I'll send along messengers to keep Glenlyon apprised of Ramsay's movements. They willna be taken unawares, lass, I promise ye."

Rose wanted to argue but he made some sense. Some. She sat back with a huff. "Fine. But I don't like it."

William scowled at that. "Ye dinna have to like it, lass. Ye just have to do it."

Well, if that wasn't the story of her life, she didn't know what was. She could only pray that following William's lead wouldn't put her mistress in more danger.

• • •

Rose slept fitfully on the pallet William had set up in the corner. He gallantly slept on a blanket stretched across the doorway. She didn't think either of them got much sleep. By the time the sun arose, her eyes were sandy and raw.

They went about preparing for the morning in silence. There was much to discuss, but Rose didn't have the energy for the arguments that would probably ensue. Neither of them would change their minds. She still thought at least one of them—preferably her—should leave. He would still want to stay to gather more information. Of which she saw the value. But the desire to protect her mistress beat through her with an urgency she couldn't ignore. She belonged at Lady Alice's side. She'd simply have to wait for an opening to escape them all.

William produced a loaf of bread and a few lumps of cheese to break their fast. Then Rose watched as he strapped on his sword and pulled on his boots.

"What now?" she asked, since he didn't seem to feel the need to share his plans.

He glanced up at her. "I have tasks to attend to." He pulled on another boot. "And, since I canna let ye out of my sight, ye'll be accompanying me."

She scowled at that and managed to bite her tongue for all of two seconds before everything erupted. "You could let me go. You know now I'm not your enemy. I could still help if I could get back home…"

But William was already shaking his head with a long-suffering look on his face. "Yer reappearance would only cause more problems. They would ask questions to which ye dinna have the answers. And that's assuming ye'd make it back on yer own."

She glared at him, but he ignored her. "As it is, ye're most likely assumed to be with yer mistress, which not only will bring her parents some measure of comfort, thinking that their daughter is with someone familiar who can care for her, but it also lends an air of respectability to her disappearance. If she were to return it could be said that ye'd never left her side. However, if ye were to return without her then the world would ken that the lady had run off on her own. Her reputation would never survive."

Rose frowned. "Her reputation will never survive, in any case. But if I were to go back perhaps I could ease their fears somewhat. At the very least, I could find out what is happening and what their plans are and if they've heard anything as to where Lady Alice has gone. Maybe they could send a warning to your laird, or…"

Again, William shook his head. "A warning has already been sent. My messenger left an hour ago. I wouldna be permitted to escort ye back regardless."

Rose rolled her eyes at that. "I could go on my own."

William snorted. "Ye have no idea where ye are and

no idea how to return. And a lassie traveling on her own, especially in these parts, wouldna make it far. These roads are far too dangerous."

"Probably because of your little band of mercenaries," she muttered.

"Aye," he said with half a grin. "And even if ye were to leave now, after the great ruckus that was caused last night by your appearance and the fact that a man died so I could keep ye with me, yer leaving now would cause more problems for me than I care to deal with."

The reminder of Roger's death sobered her, but she couldn't quite let her argument go. "You wouldn't have any of these problems if you'd left me alone to begin with."

"Aye, so ye've pointed out. Repeatedly. But as I canna go back and rectify my poor decision, we are stuck with each other for the time being. So, ye'll stay right where ye are, and I'd appreciate not hearing another word about it."

Rose glared at him and put her hand in her pocket to feel for her dagger. Not that she intended on using it on him. Yet. But holding it in her hand made her feel a little better.

However, when she felt in her pockets she found nothing but a bit of fluff and a few crumbs. She glanced up at him, eyes wide with surprise, only to glare again as he chuckled.

"If I must leave ye again, I'll return it to ye. But I have no intention of allowing you to shove that wee blade in my back the moment it's turned."

She stomped her foot in frustration, something she hadn't done since she was a small child. But the man was so unbearably aggravating she couldn't contain the slight temper tantrum.

William only chuckled again, but before he could say another word, footsteps echoed up the hallway and Lionel appeared. He nodded at each of them, his beady eyes taking everything in. When he spoke, it was directed at William.

"Mr. Ramsay will be waiting for his breakfast. Your woman is expected in the kitchens."

William opened his mouth to argue, but Lionel held up his hand. "You are needed in the armory. We leave at first light tomorrow, and Mr. Ramsay wants everything in order."

William's jaw visibly clenched, but his only response was a jerky nod of his head. Lionel's gaze briefly flicked to Rose before leaving.

William turned back to her, his eyes dark with anger, but he didn't argue with Lionel's orders. Instead, he pulled her dagger from his belt and pressed it into her hand. "Keep that well hidden but near at hand. I dinna think ye'll need it but best to be prepared."

"Will I be in danger?" she asked, icy dread nagging at her.

He shook his head. "Ye'll be in the kitchens with the other women, and the men should all be busy with preparations for the morn. Keep yer eyes and ears open, aye?"

Rose nodded and, after another moment's hesitation, William took her hand and led her to where she'd be working for the day. There were three other women in the kitchens. They didn't do much more than give her a cursory look-over and then point her to some dough to knead. With the heat of the ovens and quiet companionship of the other women, the atmosphere was almost cozy.

Still, Rose watched William walk away with a sinking feeling in her gut. He might be the reason she was in this predicament in the first place, but he was also the only one she felt even marginally safe with in this hellhole.

What a depressing thought.

At the midday meal, Rose was sent to help serve Ramsay's table. She kept an eye out for William, but whatever he was doing must have kept him too busy to eat, as he never appeared.

She walked behind the men with a jug of ale, reaching out to pour for anyone who raised their cup. She tried not to glower too much at any of them. The last thing she wanted was attention on her. She tried to make herself as unobtrusive as possible and kept her ears out for any information she could gather. So far, they hadn't said much of consequence. And then one name stood out. She stood a little closer to the table, ears straining.

"The Chivers' household is still in an uproar," a man said. Rose thought his name was Lionel. She hadn't paid too much attention earlier.

"Is that so?" Ramsay asked.

Rose's heart pounded, and she leaned over to refill Ramsay's cup though she had done so only a few minutes before.

"Yes, sir," Lionel said. "The Lady Alice has been missing a full day now and they have no idea where she might have gone or why, according to one of the maids I met in town." He chuckled. "Her maid is also missing."

Rose's heart slammed against her rib cage and she stepped back, certain they could hear it. She kept her head down, praying none of the men noticed her.

"Is she now?" Ramsay said. "That's interesting."

"Agreed," Lionel said. "The lady hasn't had any other visitors we are aware of, except for MacGregor's man, the one she visited the morning after the ball."

"*Hmm*," Ramsay said with a lecherous grin. "Yes, it was quite interesting when she popped up at the boardinghouse."

"She wasn't in there long," someone else chimed in. "Mayhap he doesn't have the stamina to keep her longer."

The men around the table laughed, but Ramsay frowned. "Or they were plotting their escape," he said. "An escape we might have discovered sooner if we'd been watching her properly from the beginning." He threw down the bread he'd been crumbling between his fingers. "I want the names of the men who were set to watching Lady Alice. If she knew where to find MacGregor, then they had to have met up before that. Had their liaison been discovered earlier, we wouldn't have been taken by surprise."

A man farther down the bench grew pale, but no one volunteered a name, and Ramsay motioned for Lionel to continue. "While we don't know when the plans were made, or the scope of them," Lionel acknowledged, "we do know Lady Alice left the inn where her family is lodging early yesterday morning. She left with a maid and several trunks, but no one else."

Rose froze again at that, but no one seemed to connect her to the woman who'd been seen with Lady Alice. She and Alice had both tried to keep their faces covered with hats and scarves to mask their identities as much as possible, in case there were anyone watching. Apparently, that had been a good plan.

"She arrived at one of the ships in port," Lionel continued. "MacGregor boarded the same ship a few hours later, and both were aboard when it set sail. We can only assume the blackguard absconded with the lady."

Ramsay nodded, a cruel smile on his face. "The MacGregors do have a nasty habit of running off with our fine English ladies."

Rose bit her cheek to keep her face from showing any emotion. According to William, Ramsay himself was Scottish, for all that he took pains to hide it.

He swallowed down a large gulp of ale and shook his head. "If it had been only MacGregor, we couldn't have been sure he'd lead us to the bastard we chase. But with the Chivers girl accompanying him that makes it more certain. Her fast friendship with the whore that highwayman stole makes their destination a near certainty. Finally, we've got them," he said with an air of intense satisfaction.

Rose didn't stay to hear more. She'd heard enough. Ramsay knew Lady Alice was with Philip, and he knew they were going to John and Elizabet. She and William had to warn them.

Now.

Chapter Six

William was kept busy throughout the day as small groups of men filtered in and out of the armory. Some needed repairs, while others needed to be totally outfitted. William had no idea where Ramsay had obtained the means to ensure every one of his men was equipped to fight, but he had. Most of the men had surely come with their own weapons. But there were a large number who seemed little more than farmers. Ramsay must either be paying them well or had some other sway over them. Knowing Ramsay, the bastard had likely recruited most of these men through threats rather than coin.

Still, William did as he was bid and tried to keep his ears open for any useful information. As the day drew on, he found his mind straying more and more to Rose. He'd made excuses several times to run errands that would bring him near to the kitchens so he could check on her. As far as he could tell, she was in no danger. But he didn't like her out of his sight, and not only because he feared for her. He had no doubt the woman would run if she got half a chance. Especially after what she'd overheard at the midday meal.

When he'd stopped by the kitchens to grab a bite to eat, she'd cornered him, insisting they leave immediately. He pointed out that they were already aware that Ramsay knew about Lady Alice and that he'd already sent a warning to Glenlyon didn't help. Only the threat of bringing more attention to her and their true reason for being with Ramsay's men kept Rose from causing a scene. He had to make her see reason and make her understand they wouldn't be any help to anyone without useful information. They could do more good keeping an eye on Ramsay than if they ran to Glenlyon. Then they'd be as much in the dark as their friends.

Still, by nightfall, he hadn't learned much more than what he already knew, and his frustration with the situation grew. The men were preparing to leave in the morning. Ramsay hadn't specified a destination but William already knew where they'd be headed. What he needed to know was specifics on what would happen once they arrived.

Finally, the last man left the armory, and William made his way back to the kitchens.

Rose glanced up as he entered, and the tension he'd carried with him all day eased. She seemed well. Covered in flour and obviously tired and frustrated, but well. She ushered him into a corner by the hearth and handed him a bowl of stew and a hunk of bread and then went back to her duties.

He watched her as she cleaned up the kitchen with the other women. She'd obviously made friends during the day. She laughed easily with them as they chatted. He liked the sound, a throaty chuckle that echoed in his chest and brought a smile to his lips. She met his gaze once and quickly looked away, but not before a becoming blush spread across her cheeks. Interesting. Perhaps she didn't hate him as much as she let on.

By the time he'd finished eating, she was ready to go.

"Did ye eat, lass?" he asked as she took his bowl.

She nodded. "I had something earlier."

He stood, much closer to her than necessary, judging by the surprised look she gave him. But they were supposed to be lovers, after all. A story that would never work if she jerked away from him every time he tried to touch her.

He brushed a lock of hair behind her ear and leaned closer, his lips brushing against her cheek. Her body stiffened against his before melting into him. Good. They needed to maintain their ruse. His instant response to her soft body pressed against his was only natural. She was an attractive woman and he was a man who had been alone for far too long. Nothing more. It had nothing to do with the slightly floral scent that was uniquely hers that seemed to intoxicate him. He drew her closer to him only because their audience would expect such behavior. Not because his arms ached to wrap around her every time he was within a few feet of her. His interest in her was only in how she could further his mission. Nothing more.

She rubbed her cheek against his, and he closed his eyes, biting back a groan. And reminded himself again of his mission. And their motives. She didn't mean her actions as anything other than a deception and responding to them like they were anything more would be a mistake. A dangerous one.

He glanced at the other women who smirked knowingly in their direction but left them be.

"Did ye hear anything interesting today?" he murmured in her ear, forcing himself to concentrate on the matter at hand and not on the nearly overwhelming urge to tilt her face up so he could claim those full, pouty lips.

She gave him a quick nod. "When we're alone," she said, her voice barely more than a whisper.

He kept her elbow in his hand as he led her out of the kitchens. Then he wrapped his arm about her, pulling her close. She started to push away from him until they passed one of the men who'd leered at her before. She glared at him and sank back against William. William kept them moving but rested his other hand on the hilt of his sword. The man scowled, but turned away, obviously receiving the message. Rose stayed tucked against William's side until they made it to his quarters.

She moved away the moment they were safely inside, and he shoved aside the inexplicable disappointment. She wasn't really his. In fact, she was the embodiment of possibly the worst mistake he'd ever made. The sooner they parted ways the better. He had no business wanting to be near her.

"Did ye discover anything useful today?" he asked, keeping his attention on anything but her.

A faint frown creased her brow, and she sank onto the stool by the small fire he had going in the ruined hearth. "The man called Lionel…"

William nodded so she continued. "He saw me—a maid, he said—with Lady Alice on the docks. But neither he nor any of the other men have shown any sign that they know it was me," she said quickly before William could react.

"Good. That's good."

"Yes, it's good they didn't recognize me but not that they had men watching Lady Alice's home. And they were watching your kinsman as well. Did you know that?"

He sighed and rubbed his face. "No. I suspected as much, but no. I wasna privy to that information, and that concerns me."

It concerned him a great deal. Not that there had been men watching. They'd assumed as much, even if they'd hoped otherwise. And there was naught to do about it now. But the fact that men had been set to watch and William hadn't been told about it was troubling. The whole reason he was with Ramsay was to spy. To ingratiate himself with the enemy and earn a position of importance so he would be privy to such plans. He didn't appear to be doing a good job. He'd never forgive himself if some lack on his part resulted in harm coming to his kinsmen.

Rose's brow was furrowed and he waved it off, trying to set her mind at ease. "Let's not worry about that now. As long as they dinna recognize ye, we should be safe."

She didn't look like she totally agreed, but she nodded.

"Did you hear anything else useful?"

"I don't know if it's useful or not, but interesting, at least."

"What is?"

"They kept me baking all day, long past the time I'd expected to be released."

"That's no' so unusual when there's a large group of men to feed, is it?"

"Perhaps not. But these weren't the larger loaves of bread I'd expect to make for a...household such as this. But smaller loaves and cakes."

"Travel rations," William said, and Rose nodded.

"I believe so. And small groups of men kept stopping in all day. Again, not unusual for men to steal through the kitchen throughout the day, looking for a bite to eat. But these were more organized groups. It happened three or four times. And they weren't stealing a cake here or there. Mrs. Bradshaw, the head cook, was handing each a small parcel."

William sat on the other chair with a sigh. "Aye, that fits with what I saw in the armory today. Small groups of men coming by here and there between the regular visits I'd expect for repairs and new weapons."

"Is it important, do you think?"

William shrugged. "Maybe so, maybe no. It's no secret we are marching out at dawn tomorrow. The men will need food and supplies."

"Well, yes, but wouldn't they get those things anyway

when we stopped to camp for the night?"

"Aye," he said with a frown. Finally, he shook his head. "There's naught we can do about it tonight. Let's get some rest. We leave early in the morning, and we'll need our wits about us."

They bedded down for the night, with Rose taking William's cot while he again guarded the door.

Rose settled into his blankets with a sigh. A few moments later she loosed a mumbled curse, and William chuckled under his breath.

"How did you take it this time?" she asked, having obviously realized her dagger was no longer in her pocket.

"I'll give it back to ye in the morning."

"If you are going to give it back to me anyway, what's the harm in letting me have it now?"

"I'm about to rest my tired head. The last thing I wish is to awake with yer wee blade at my throat. Now go to sleep."

She muttered again, something about damn Scots and other surely shocking things, before she finally settled down. He quietly laughed again and lay down. She might be the biggest pain in the arse he'd ever been saddled with, but at least she kept things amusing.

. . .

The first day of traveling had Rose so bone-weary by the end of the day she'd have happily slept in a pigsty. So, when they came upon an isolated farmstead, warm light glowing from the windows, she greeted the sight with delight. Perhaps they'd get a decent night's sleep after all, if the owner was amenable to being hospitable.

She frowned when William cursed under his breath.

"What's wrong? Afraid the owners won't have room for everyone and you'll have to sleep out in the cold again?" she teased.

But William didn't smile. His mouth hardened. "I'm afraid they willna be given the choice."

All amusement drained from Rose, replaced by a crushing dread. Oh, dear heavens. He wouldn't...

Before she could even finish the thought, Ramsay was motioning several of his men forward, including William. Rose opened her mouth, but William flashed her a look that commanded silence and she snapped it closed again, for once not hesitating to obey. The look on his face brooked no argument. His features were hard, determined. And terrifying. Yet somehow, she didn't fear him. And she couldn't imagine him actually hurting the people inside that farmhouse.

She held back with the other women, her hands clenching into fists when the screams started. It was over within minutes. Some of the other men exited the house, laughing and congratulating one another on a job well done. Rose swallowed convulsively against the bile rising in her throat.

Her eyes scanned the group for William, but he wasn't among them. Her heart hammered painfully in her chest. Where was he?

The rest of the group moved forward, taking over the farmstead. The women were sent into the kitchen to prepare food. Rose tried not to see the wreckage of the house. Though there was actually less damage than she'd have imagined. The poor people who lived here must not have been able to put up much of a fight. The absence of blood soothed her somewhat. But she still hadn't seen Will.

She finally got up the courage to ask one of the men if he'd seen him.

He snorted. "Butler's the one who did in the ol' biddy what lived here. So, we told 'im it were his job to get rid of 'er. 'Es probably still out back buryin' 'er."

The blood drained from Rose's face so quickly the room spun. She forced herself to nod at the man and then excused herself. She needed some air. And she needed to find Will.

She'd taken only a few steps outside when he rounded the corner of the barn. She stood stock-still, letting him come to her. Part of her wanted to scream, hit him, berate him for the vile thing he'd just done. And she would have. If she could fully believe it. But she couldn't. No matter what she'd been told, she couldn't believe he'd do something so horrible.

When he saw her, he hastened his pace, reaching her in a few long strides. He stopped a few inches from her, gripping her arms tight.

"Rose. Are ye well, lass? What's the matter?"

"You didn't…tell me you didn't…"

He shook his head and glanced around, making sure they were alone. Then he leaned in and spoke so quietly none would hear but she if there were anyone lurking about. "The house was inhabited only by an old widow. I did hit her—"

Rose jerked in his arms, and he tightened his grip. "That bastard Gerard was about to run her through with his sword. I did what I had to. But I swear to ye, I was as soft as I could be. When she fell I leaned over to grab her and told her to play dead and carried her outside."

Some of the tension in Rose dissipated, but her gaze darted about the yard, looking for some sign of the woman. All she saw was a faint mound of dirt under a tree near the backside of the barn.

"Then where is she?" she asked, not sure she wanted to know the answer.

"I gave her some money and directions to Glenlyon, along with a message for Malcolm. She'll be well looked after there."

Rose sagged into William's arms, relief flooding her. "I knew you were a good man," she murmured.

William chuckled. "I wouldna go that far, but I do try to make my mam proud."

She buried her face against his chest and breathed deep. A fine tremor ran through her body, and he pulled her closer.

"Hey, lass. Dinna fash now. I'm here." He pressed a kiss to the top of her head. "Though I didna think ye cared so much," he said, his voice thick with amusement.

She laughed, though the sound was shaky. "Let's just say, it's been a very long night."

"Aye. That it has. Let's get some sleep, shall we?"

She pulled back from him a little. "I'm supposed to be helping in the kitchens."

He shrugged. "And I'm supposed to be burying an old woman in the woods."

That startled another laugh out of her, and he grinned. "Come then, lass. I dinna think anyone will be looking for us tonight."

He took her hand and led her toward a small building near the barn. Judging by the smell the place was likely used as a smoke shed, but Rose didn't care. It was warm and quiet. And with Will at her side, it was safe. And for the first time, she didn't shrink from him when he lay by her side.

She couldn't guarantee she would feel the same the next time he slept beside her. But for that night, she welcomed his arms around her.

They left early the next morning and continued traveling north. They thankfully didn't come upon any other remote farms. In fact, nothing noteworthy happened. The days blended into one another. But the nights were another matter entirely.

Chapter Seven

The next two weeks were spent traveling at a snail's pace across England and into Scotland with Ramsay and his men. William sent off two more messengers to Glenlyon, letting their friends know of Ramsay's movements and location as best as they could. Still, Rose's trepidation grew the farther into Scottish territory they traveled. As did her homesickness. She'd traveled with her lady, of course. But they'd always traveled with their household between the Chivers' estates. Rose had never been so far from home before. And never with the possibility she might not return.

The land grew wilder, and, while it was far more beautiful than she'd ever expected, it was also very remote. There were large cities, of course, but none so grand as London, she was sure. But Ramsay kept his men to the woodlands and back trails so as to avoid the attention of any other travelers. Which meant when night fell, they slept in the heather instead of in a nice, warm bed. But Rose preferred that, uncomfortable as it was, to raiding another farm. She both looked forward to the night and dreaded it. It was good to stop walking and be able to rest. Of course, she must help prepare meals and ensure Ramsay had everything he needed before she could go to her bed, such as it was. But it was heavenly to lie back and close her eyes.

Or it would have been. Except for William, who still insisted on sharing her sleeping space. She understood the need for it. It both kept up appearances that she was his woman and allowed him to protect her throughout the night. But she'd never slept with a man before. And certainly not one as...appealing as William. It was disconcerting, to say the least.

The first night after leaving the farm, when he'd joined her in her bedroll and wrapped his arms about her, she'd lain so stiffly that he'd finally leaned over and pressed featherlight kisses up her neck. She squirmed, but he held her fast.

"If ye dinna stop acting like ye're afraid I'll eat ye up the moment ye close yer eyes, we'll never convince anyone ye belong to me."

"That's because I *don't* belong to you," she said, though she did make a concerted effort to stop cringing from him.

"Aye, but we need them to think ye do, remember? At least stop acting like ye hate me."

She tried to relax in his arms. "I don't hate you."

"Do ye no'?" he asked, his voice genuinely surprised.

She snorted. "You might not be my favorite person. You did kidnap me, after all."

"Aye," he sighed. "So ye keep reminding me."

"But no, I don't hate you. And I do appreciate you going through so much trouble to keep me safe."

He chuckled and pulled her closer. "Ah, lass. It's no' so much trouble to lie with a beautiful woman."

Her stomach skittered and flipped, and a fine tremble ran through her limbs. She'd never had a man say such things to her before.

"Are ye cold?" he asked, snuggling even closer so he could wrap his blanket about them both.

She wasn't. But she didn't say anything to dissuade him. If she was stuck sleeping in the dirt with this marauding band of mercenaries, she would rather do so wrapped in the arms of the handsome Highlander than take her chances with the other men whose eyes followed her. With William at her back and the fire guarding their front, she felt as safe as she could be in the circumstances.

Each night he came to her. And each night she grew more and more comfortable sleeping wrapped in his arms. That didn't mean she forgave him. But there were definite advantages to having him as a bedfellow. Not the least of which his presence in her bed made his presence in her waking hours less jarring. A necessity when the success of their subterfuge depended upon their familiarity with each other. She no longer cringed when he reached out to touch her in some small way; to tuck a strand of hair behind her ear or gently caress her cheek.

She even managed to laugh along with the others when he'd swat at her bottom when she'd walk by or made some crude joke at her expense. The only thing that still rattled her was when he'd pull her close for a quick kiss when he'd pass her in the camp. But it wasn't because she was uncomfortable with his touch. No. It was much more sinister than that.

She'd begun to crave it.

She didn't have to pretend that she enjoyed it when he wrapped his arms about her. When his lips pressed against hers, hungering, demanding…she didn't have to pretend for the camp anymore. More and more, it was herself she had to lie to. She liked it far too much. Wanted it. Had even found herself seeking him out throughout the day just so she could pass by and create an opportunity for a little playacting.

Even worse, she was fairly sure William was doing the

same thing. He seemed to find inane excuses to seek her out during the day. And without fail, those visits would end with a kiss that stole her breath. And her sanity. They couldn't keep on this way. And yet they must.

But she resolved to strengthen her internal defenses against him. He was the enemy. The epitome of every terrifying story she'd been told of the savage Scots who lived and died by their swords. The man had kidnapped her, for goodness sake! He was, by his own admission, a thief, a highwayman, and now a mercenary for the devil himself. It was *that* which she must keep foremost in her mind. Not the way his fingers felt brushing against her skin. Or the way his full lips seemed to burn from within, their heat branding her anew with every kiss they shared.

She blew out a pent-up breath and leaned over the fire she'd been tending to give the stew simmering over it a stir. When she looked up, she caught William's gaze on her. She froze, locked in place by the intensity of his stare. A slow smile stretched over his lips that sent her stomach into a free fall. She choked on the small gasp that caught in her throat. She must fight this!

She stood straighter and glared at him, then turned her back, the sound of his laughter following her. The man was aggravating, but they had bigger problems.

Men were disappearing from the camp.

Over the course of their journey, more and more men went missing.

Well, not missing exactly. Ramsay didn't seem at all displeased or troubled as small groups of men—two or three here, four or five there—peeled off from the main group and disappeared. Rose mentioned it to William when she saw three men wander off after a rest stop, but he didn't seem concerned.

"It's actually quite clever," he said, though he looked like he didn't want to admit it.

"Clever?" she asked.

"Aye." He nodded absently and took a bite of the hard trail rations she'd brought him. They'd stayed at this camp for several days now, and many of the men were growing antsy. So was Rose. She knew they must be near Glenlyon, and the need to protect her mistress from impending danger burned through her.

William took another bite, glancing around before continuing. "Traveling with such a large group is suspicious, which is why we've been keeping off the main roads and trails. Sending small groups of men ahead not only reduces the main body of our group, but it allows Ramsay to scout ahead and position men in different areas."

Rose put her hands on her hips, both frightened at the implications and grudgingly admiring of the tactic. "So they can move ahead, faster than the main group, and be in position to attack before we ever get near Glenlyon."

"Aye. And there lies our main problem."

Rose frowned at him. "What?"

"One large group is difficult to hide. I'd be able to divulge their position without too much trouble, even if we were to leave before they reached their final destination. But several small groups? Dozens perhaps?" He shook his head. "There's no way to ken where all these men will be stationed."

She sat beside him, her soup ladle in her hand. "There must be a way to find out. Surely, Ramsay doesn't know where each of a dozen or more groups is only in his head. He must have a...map of some kind. Something to plan and mark where each group is."

"Aye," William said. "And if he has such a thing, he's

keeping it close, showing it to none but his most trusted men. Perhaps not even them."

"So how do we get a look, then?"

"That's a very good question, lass."

Rose paced back and forth in front of their small fire, not caring if anyone saw. They could think it was a lovers' quarrel for all she cared. "This is ridiculous. We should leave now. We have to warn our friends."

William looked like he wanted to pull out every hair on his head but to his credit he kept his temper. Which actually made Rose even more irritated with him. How could the man remain so calm?

"We can't leave yet, lass. We're still a day's ride from Glenlyon and, despite what we have learned, we have no way of knowing when or even *if* he will attack."

"But we have been sitting here for two days. If he was going to attack, wouldn't he have moved us closer by now? Or sent more men out? Something? He's made no move."

"Perhaps," William said. "Or perhaps he is planning something else. Which is exactly why we need to stay where we are until we can find out more details. We are only a day's ride away. The two of us can travel much quicker than Ramsay's whole mob. We'll get there in time to warn them."

"Yes, but that's the problem. Don't you see? We are only a day's ride away. If he were to order the men to march now, we wouldn't have any time to warn our friends. By the time we got there Ramsay would be right at our heels. Or worse, the men he has spread around might reach Glenlyon first. We need to leave now so they have time to prepare."

"We will leave soon, I promise ye. But without more details I wouldna even ken what to warn them about. I'll not risk more lives by acting too soon. We have always been aware that Ramsay would attack. Our friends are ready for that. And I have been sending messengers, so they willna be caught unawares. What we dinna ken is when and from what direction and how many men and all the other small details that will make the difference between winning this fight and losing."

"We've been traveling with them for nearly two weeks now," Rose said. "I don't think you're going to discover anything new that you haven't already discovered. Unless you can get in to see that map. Something I could probably do but you won't even let me try."

William sighed and tossed another log onto the flames. "Saints preserve me from inpatient women," he muttered.

"And saints preserve me from stubborn men," she said, throwing up her hands to stomp off a few feet before rounding back at him. "If we arrive too late to do any good and our friends suffer for it, I will hold you responsible, William McGregor. I'll never forgive you for it."

"Add it to the list of things ye'll never forgive me for, lass."

Rose opened her mouth to say something else, but Mrs. Bradshaw chose that moment to wander by and shoo her back to the main fire where they were ladling out food for the men. Rose threw a glare over her shoulder at him that he rolled his eyes at, and then she returned to her duties.

She had an idea. One she knew William would hate. But if they couldn't leave to warn their friends until they had more information from Ramsay, then someone was going to have to get close to him to get it.

Fear rippled through her, but she steeled her spine. Her mistress needed her. And so did the people of Glenlyon. She and William could argue over whose fault their situation was later. For the moment, there was something she could do to help and she'd do it whether he agreed or no.

She only hoped she wouldn't get killed in the process.

She grabbed a kettle of hot water from the large fire and walked straight to Ramsay's tent, head high as if she had been summoned and had every right to be entering the master's space. Her hands shook and she held tighter to the kettle, taking care to keep her apron wrapped about the handle. She prayed he would not be inside. If he was, she'd offer him the hot water for tea or to wash. And she'd try to get a look around.

When she reached the tent, she scratched at the flap that served as a door and waited a few seconds. When there was no response, she took a quick look around the camp to make sure no one was paying attention to her, and then slipped inside.

Ramsay's accommodations were luxurious compared to his men's. A large, comfortable-looking cot sat in one corner, piled high with furs and soft blankets. Candles burned merrily, giving the place a soft glow. But the item that interested her the most was the table set up in the middle of the tent. She glanced around again to be sure she'd missed no one lurking in the shadows, and then crept closer.

On top of the table was a map. She didn't recognize the area but there was a large X marked toward the center north. Scattered around that X were several smaller versions, nearly a dozen total. Excitement sent her heart skittering in her chest. Could these be the locations of Ramsay's men?

She looked around the tent again but didn't see anything she could draw with. The kettle grew heavy in her hands and she stooped to nestle it in the embers of the fire. A bit of soot from the ashes remained on her fingers and she brushed her hands against her apron, trying to clean them. And then sucked in a breath as an idea hit her.

She scooped up a bit of ash from the edges of the fire and carried it to the table. Once she'd deposited her little pile of ash near the map she twisted her apron so the backside was visible. Dipping her finger in the ash, she made a large X mark near the top center of her apron. And then she went about copying the other marks as well as she could. It wouldn't give exact locations, of course. But hopefully it would give the MacGregors at least an idea of where Ramsay's men might be lying in wait.

She finished as quickly as possible and then scooped the remaining ash into her palm and carried it back to the fire. She'd barely brushed it off into the fire when she heard a voice behind her.

She stood, whirling around. Her hands smoothed down her apron, and she forced herself not to look at it. The "map" was on the backside that rested against her skirts, so nothing should be visible except, perhaps, a bit of soot. And, since she'd been smearing her ash-covered hands on her apron, that shouldn't draw notice.

Lionel stood in the doorway, staring at her. He didn't look angry or even surprised. His lips pulled into a slow smile that didn't reach his eyes.

She dropped into a quick curtsy. "May I help you with something, sir?"

His grin grew at that, and a faint tremor of alarm ran down her spine. "Oh, there are quite a few things I'm sure you can help me with," he said. He glanced around the tent, his gaze resting on the map before returning to her. "What are you doing in Mr. Ramsay's tent?"

She knotted her hands in her skirts to keep them from shaking. "I brought him some hot water, sir," she said, pointing at the kettle resting in the fire embers and thanking the saints above she'd thought to bring it.

Lionel nodded slowly, some of the suspicion leaving his eyes. But he still didn't move from the doorway. "Well, since the master isn't here, perhaps you can assist me." His gaze flicked over her again. "It's been a while since I've had a proper wash." His hands went to the buckle of his belt and ice-cold fear flooded Rose's veins.

"I...I should be getting back to William," she said through numb lips.

"He won't miss you for a few more minutes."

"Aye, I would," William said, stepping into the tent, his sword already drawn and pointed at Lionel's throat.

Lionel smiled at him with that cold, calculating smile of his, but Rose nearly sobbed in relief. William nodded his head away from the door and Lionel obliged by moving farther into the tent. William moved with him, reaching out for Rose once he neared her. She released a sobbing gasp and grabbed his hand, letting him draw her in to his side.

She could be brave when needed, but she wasn't an idiot. She wouldn't win a duel with Lionel. And while William was aggravating and the cause of the most miserable weeks of her life, she knew he wouldn't hurt her. So bravery be damned, she clung to him for all she was worth.

And Lord bless him, he clung back.

Chapter Eight

William kept Lionel moving until he was well away from the door…their one point of escape. He didn't know what Rose had been doing in Ramsay's tent. He'd have to throttle her for that later. Right now, he needed to concentrate on getting them both out of the tent, and the camp, alive.

"What are you two plotting in here, *hmm*?" Lionel asked.

Rose kept herself behind William. The lass was headstrong and a pain in his arse, but she at least had some sense when it counted. He had no doubt she would fight like a hellcat, but there were some battles a woman wouldn't win. Having to fight her on top of their enemies would guarantee someone would get hurt.

"Plotting? My Rose was simply stopping by to make sure Mr. Ramsay didna need anything else before he retired," William said. "I'll admit I shouldna have followed but…well, ye canna blame a man for being jealous of his woman giving attention to another man."

Rose released a perfectly timed outraged gasp. Will squeezed her arm, both to comfort and praise.

Lionel took a small side step, not retreating but moving enough that William would be forced to move also to keep his sword aimed at his neck. He wouldn't be able to hold such a position for much longer anyway, so he dropped the sword a bit, though he still held it ready. "And why are ye here when Ramsay is not? I canna imagine he expects ye to hang about his tent."

"Of course not. However, since Mr. Ramsay isn't here, I thought it best to see why your...lady lingered."

William frowned at that. "Have ye been following her?"

"Yes, as a matter of fact. You, as well."

William's hand clenched on the hilt of his sword. Apparently, they were no longer keeping up appearances. But that didn't mean he would openly admit to anything.

"Why would ye be doing that?" William asked.

"Don't you know?" Lionel said, eyebrows raised in mock surprise. "Let me enlighten you. I wasn't quite truthful with our master when I told him that I didn't recognize the maid on the dock. And yes, I noticed you paying extra attention to that bit of the conversation," he said, pointing to Rose.

Then he got a thoughtful look on his face. "Well, I suppose I wasn't being untruthful. At the time, I didn't recognize your pretty little plaything," he said with a sneer at Rose. "Until you walked into camp with her. That face isn't one I would forget anytime soon," he said with a leer that sent a bolt of rage crashing through William.

Rose shrank back behind him, and he put a hand out to keep her close. He'd need it when it came down to the fight that was coming, but right then, he needed the contact with her more.

"I dinna ken yer meaning."

"Oh, I'm certain you do." Lionel shifted his gaze to where Rose peeked out behind William and pointed to her. "It was you that day that I saw watching the ship. And why would you be watching the ship unless your mistress had boarded it? What is most interesting is that it was the same ship that Philip MacGregor sailed out on. And then a few hours later, our William brought you into our camp. Now what reason could there be for that?"

She clung to his arm, but her voice was strong when she answered. "William is my intended, sir. My mistress gave me leave to join him, as she had no more need of my services. There's nothing more to the story than that."

Lionel shook his head, a cruel smile playing on his lips. "I do not believe you."

"What do ye want, Lionel?" William said, cutting to the chase.

He shrugged. "I was curious, that's all. I found it very... interesting that she, with what I know of her, is lurking about in our master's tent. And you were right on her heels. As I knew you'd be."

"And what reason would we have for lurking, as ye say?" William already knew his answer. But he needed time to come up with a plan that would get him and Rose out of that tent unharmed. The odds of doing so while leaving Lionel unscathed were rapidly disappearing.

"Why?" Lionel laughed. "A Scot with a vague background and a maid whose mistress is a MacGregor whore? Why else would you be here but to spy?"

William had known such an accusation would come his way eventually. Frankly, he was surprised it had taken so long once Rose had joined him. Still, he had no intention of admitting such a thing.

"Oh? And have ye told Ramsay of yer suspicions? I'd hate to see ye punished when ye're proven wrong."

Lionel chuckled. "You're worth your mettle, I'll give you that. Such dedication to the role you play." He slapped his hand against his thigh a few times, dragging out the suspense until William had to clench his hands into fists to keep from twitching.

"No. I haven't shared what I've learned. Yet. I generally find it best to keep information to myself until I know how it will best serve my purposes."

William nodded, his finger straying toward his dagger as unobtrusively as possible as Lionel moved closer. There wasn't anywhere else for William to go. He and Rose were backed up against the wall of the tent. He didn't like the way Lionel watched them, looking for an opening to attack.

"Well," William said, trying to move Rose to the side. Lionel kept the same distance between them but didn't stop them from hedging toward the door. What was he up to? "I hate to disappoint ye, but as I said, Rose couldna have been the woman ye saw on the docks. And even if she was—"

William lunged for him, but Lionel was ready and managed to dodge William's thrust. He spun, slashing out with his right hand that William noticed too late held a dagger. The blade sliced into his arm. Not deep, but his hand went numb momentarily, and he dropped his sword.

Lionel raised his own sword, triumph blazoned on his face.

Then there was a sickening crunch, and Lionel's eyes widened. He staggered forward, clutching his head, to reveal Rose standing behind him holding a candlestick.

"Here!" she said, holding out her dagger.

Why that little…when had she taken that back?

She tossed it to him and he caught it, turned, and plunged it into Lionel's chest, piercing his lung. Lionel's mouth opened in a soundless scream before he slowly slumped to the ground. Rose dropped the candlestick and pressed her hands to her mouth.

William turned to her, grasping her arms. "Are ye hurt?"

She shook her head. She seemed dazed, but he didn't see

any wounds or obvious injuries.

As soon as he'd assured himself she was unharmed, he knelt over Lionel and pulled the blade from his chest, wiping it off on Lionel's shirt.

"Well, lass. It looks like ye've got yer wish," William said.

Rose looked at him, her brow furrowed.

"We canna stay here now. He might not be able to tell Ramsay about us, but Ramsay *will* notice his absence. And I've no doubt others witnessed the three of us entering this tent. When only two of us depart…"

"We're done for," she said.

He nodded. "We leave. Tonight. We need to hide him first," he said, pointing to Lionel's body.

He took the dagger and cut a slash in the corner of the tent. "Grab something to wrap around him," he said.

She yanked a blanket from the bed and tossed it to him. Between the two of them, they wrapped the blanket around the man and hauled him out. They obscured him the best they could in the woods behind the tent, but it wouldn't fool anyone for long.

"That will have to do. We must leave. Now," he said.

"Wait," she said, ducking back into the tent.

He cursed but followed her back inside. "We must leave," he said.

"A moment, please." She quickly pulled a rug over the bloodstain on the ground and then glanced around. Apparently, everything was to her satisfaction because she nodded her head once and then took off her apron, folding it quickly and shoving it into her bag.

William had found himself cursing her more often than not since he'd had the misfortune of taking her. But in that moment, he felt only pride and approval at how she was handling the whole situation.

"Come," he said, taking her hand. She didn't question

him nor did she give in to the panic that he saw lurking in her eyes. Instead, she took his hand and let him lead her into the night.

· · ·

William took her hand and walked her quickly to their fire. A few men looked in their direction, and he muttered something in Gaelic that Rose was pretty sure she was glad she didn't understand. Then he pulled her to his side, burying his nose in her hair.

Her heart skipped into her throat at his sudden amorous attentions, so it took her a second to understand what he was saying.

"Laugh," he said.

"Are you crazy?" she managed to say.

"We need to look like we dinna have a care in the world, lass. Like we're about to go back to our little fire so I can have my way with ye."

Her heart pounded anew. And at the way his breath tickled at her neck. The way his arms held her tight. She needed it right then. Needed him. To drown out the horror she'd witnessed.

But she had no time to sink in to him. To let him comfort her. Or to wish his words had any hint of reality. She had to pretend to be in love. So they could escape before they were discovered.

"That might be difficult with your arm bleeding all over everything."

He laughed for real at that, and she forced a giggle.

"Aye, I suppose I'll need to see to that sooner or later. For now, let's concentrate on getting out of here alive."

She hung on William, hoping it looked as if she hadn't a care in the world when really her legs were about to give out from under her. She'd clobbered a man over the head with a candlestick and then watched him be stabbed to death. And helped hide his body. Definitely not what she'd expected when she'd slipped into that tent.

William steered her back to their fire and tumbled her onto the blankets. He kept his back to the main group, hiding their movements as they gathered their saddlebags, shoving inside the few possessions they'd left out.

"We're going to wrap these blankets about us and get to my horse as quickly and quietly as possible."

"Wait."

"We canna wait, lass. What is it?"

She reached under her skirt and ripped a strip from her petticoat. "We won't get far if you leave a blood trail so thick even that drunken lot could follow it."

She wrapped it around his arm and tied it off, tight. "I'll do a better job once we get away, but that might keep you from bleeding to death in the meantime."

William snorted. "My thanks. Are ye ready?"

She nodded, thankful he'd had the foresight to keep his horse separate from the others. There were a few laughs and jeers as they stumbled away from their small fire, but no one questioned their sudden desire for privacy.

She tried to follow him with limbs that had gone numb from shock. He quickly untied his horse and grabbed her around the waist, boosting her up. She scrambled to stay on the horse's back while William climbed up behind her and took the reins.

"Hold on, lass," he said, kicking the horse into a run. But he didn't go in the direction that they had been traveling.

"Where are we going?" Rose asked.

"The last thing we want to do is lead them straight to Glenlyon."

"But they already know where it is," she said over her

shoulder.

"Aye, but they dinna ken that we are connected with them. Right now, all they'll suspect is that I killed one of our men. But they willna ken why. If we're caught headed in the direction of Glenlyon, it willna be hard to put two and two together. So, we'll have to take a more circuitous route."

"Why didn't we take two horses?"

"Because I dinna wish to be branded a horse thief along with traitor and murderer. They canna hang me for taking my own horse," he said not bothering to keep the sarcasm from his voice.

"Yes, but wouldn't we travel faster with two?"

William huffed. "Possibly. Then again, I can keep a much closer eye on ye when ye're in my arms."

She couldn't stop the shiver that ran through her, and he tightened his arms about her.

"Besides," he continued, "taking my own horse willna seem too suspicious. Hopefully, they'll only assume I've gone off on some mission like the other men who have been leaving. If two horses were to disappear, however, it would raise questions, especially as we'd have to steal ye one. With only one horse gone they canna be sure if ye're with me or no' or if we're still together. I might have deserted or ye might have wandered off. They might even think Lionel has dragged ye off for a bit of fun, which will hide his disappearance for a bit longer. The point being, it lends an air of confusion that will only be in our benefit."

Rose didn't say anything more after. With William hell-bent on putting as much distance between them and Ramsay's camp as possible, she felt it more prudent to concentrate on staying on the horse. Once they got into thicker trees, however, it was necessary for them to slow down. It was too dark and dangerous for them to travel quickly.

"Shouldn't we stop?" Rose said. "I want to get there as

soon as possible, but I'd like to reach my mistress alive. We can't see anything in the dark."

"No," William said, weaving the horse through another thicket of trees along a trail that Rose couldn't see. "We need to get as far away as we can, and it will be easier for them to lose our trail in the thick underbrush here. We must put a fair bit of distance between us before we can circle back around and continue on toward Glenlyon."

"But it's dangerous to travel in the dark."

William chuckled. "Nay, lass. Dinna fash. I know these lands well. We are not so far from Glenlyon, in fact. I have traveled through these woods many a time. Ye can rest if ye'd like. I willna let ye fall."

She snorted softly. "I'd appreciate that." She sat silently for all of two minutes before she started questioning him again.

"Once Lionel's body is discovered along with your absence, they will surely determine you are a traitor to their cause," Rose said, "and possibly a MacGregor to boot."

"A reasonable assumption."

"Then it also stands to reason that they'll know you'll head straight for Glenlyon. They might speed up their timeline and come sooner, perhaps right on our heels. It seems our purposes would be better served if we get ourselves to Glenlyon as quickly as possible rather than wasting time trying to fool them."

"Perhaps. But as I've told ye before, Glenlyon is well aware of the threat Ramsay presents and my kinsmen are vigilant in watching for him. So we willna be going to Glenlyon."

Rose twisted in the saddle at that and looked at him with wide eyes. "But we must warn them!"

William gave her a sharp nod. "Aye, we will. But it is not the Lion of Glenlyon who is in danger. It is my Laird John and his lady. And they do not dwell at Glenlyon, but at

Kirkenroch."

"What? Why did you never tell me this?"

"I wasna sure I could trust ye. It's not knowledge I commonly share with those I *do* trust."

"So you trust me now?"

"I didna say that," he said, his voice tinged with amusement. "But as I'm taking ye there now it seems to be a moot point."

"Then Lady Alice…"

"Aye, she'll likely be there with them. We must go there first and warn them, and then we can send a message to Glenlyon."

"Does Ramsay know of Kirkenroch?" Rose asked.

William shook his head. "I dinna think so. Which is why I've taken care to hide our trail. I dinna wish to betray its location."

"But will Ramsay not go to Glenlyon first then? Putting them in the greatest danger?"

"Aye. But Glenlyon is a heavily fortified castle with half the clan residing within its walls. It is well defended and, as I said, already on guard against enemies. Kirkenroch is little more than a ruin with naught but my laird's family and some loyal workers living there. Should Ramsay ride to the gates of Glenlyon he would find battle-ready men marching out to meet him. But John and his lady…" He shook his head again. "Nay. We must warn them first. Kirkenroch is not such a great distance from Glenlyon. Sending a rider there once we reach them will be sufficient. But we must warn John first. He is who Ramsay hunts."

Rose nodded slowly. "How soon will we get there? I fear for my lady."

"We should arrive tomorrow if we ride hard through the night. Can ye do that, lass?"

Rose sat straighter in the saddle and nodded her head. "I

can do what I must. Whatever is necessary in order to reach my lady before it is too late."

William tightened his arms about her, ignoring the twinge in his wounded arm as another swell of pride replaced his usual irritation with her. She had more courage, strength, and determination than most men he knew.

She did well, gallantly clinging to the horse despite the exhaustion he knew sapped her strength. But a few hours before dawn he knew they must stop for rest. Her head nodded as she tried not to fall asleep. And his arm ached. He flexed it a little and swayed in the saddle at the sudden light-headedness that hit him.

They needed to stop. Soon.

Chapter Nine

Rose's head bobbed on her shoulders, jerking her awake once again. She looked around her surroundings. They had slowed their pace, and the horse was now picking its way carefully through the thick trees and underbrush.

"Are we close?" she asked, patting his hand to get his attention. Then she gasped. His hands were freezing cold. And she could detect a faint tremble when she took his hand in hers.

"We must stop," she said. "I think you are losing too much blood."

"Aye, we'll stop soon. A bit of a rest wouldna be amiss," he said. "The horse could use one too, I'm sure."

He tried to make his voice light, but she could hear the weariness.

"Where are we?"

"There is a place we can go, not too far ahead. We'll stop there and rest for a few hours. We are but a couple hours from Kirkenroch now but I dinna wish to arrive dragging a dead horse and half-dead maid."

Rose rolled her eyes at that. "You'll be the one half dead if I don't get your arm properly bandaged. Why didn't you stop earlier once we were out of danger? Foolish man."

He chuckled, but the weary sound didn't ease the anxious tumbling of her stomach.

They reached a clearing where the burned-out remains of a cottage was hidden among the shrubbery. It was beautiful in that hauntingly sad way ruined dwellings had.

"What is this place?" she asked.

William brought the horse up to a crumbling wall and dismounted. He reached up to help her slide down, keeping his arms about her when she stumbled. Her legs were numb from sitting astride the horse for so long, and she stretched, groaning at the crack in her back. William smiled and turned to loosely tie the horse at the wall, giving him enough lead to graze.

"This used to be the gamekeeper's cottage. I came here often as a child. It's a good place to be alone with your thoughts."

Rose cocked an eyebrow at that.

"What?" he asked.

She shrugged. "You don't seem like an overly thoughtful sort of person."

He gave her a mock glare, and she laughed. He took her hand to lead her inside. "I have four sisters," he said. "Trust me when I say, having a quiet place to escape to was priceless."

Rose nodded and looked around. "It's beautiful here. What happened to it?"

"I dinna ken. It happened a long time ago. Maybe in one of the skirmishes with the Campbell clan over the years."

Rose looked back at him sharply. "Are they still a threat?"

William frowned for a second but then shook his head. "No. After Ramsay's attack on Glenlyon, Malcolm and the Campbell chief made a truce. Between that and Malcolm's marriage to Campbell's daughter, the fighting has ceased. It's an uneasy alliance, but I think most are weary of fighting. It's been going on for centuries."

Rose raised another eyebrow at that. "What on earth did they fight over?"

William shrugged again. "Pretty much anything and everything that could possibly be fought over. Let's get inside and then I'll answer all yer questions."

She noticed anew the pallor of his face and nodded, ashamed she'd kept him outside talking when she should have been tending his arm.

William went in ahead and made sure the space was safe and unoccupied before ushering her inside. The interior wasn't much different than the first encampment they had been in with Ramsay. The cottage was little more than a stone floor and four walls. Despite the damage, it was whole for the most part, and once he had a small fire going it proved to be quite cozy.

"You must let me attend your arm," she said. William tried to wave her off but she scowled and grabbed his good arm. "You won't be any good to me or anyone else if you pass out from blood loss or lose your use of that arm. Sit down and quit being so stubborn."

He snorted at her but did as she bid. She clucked over him for a few minutes, peeling off the blood-soaked bandage that she had hastily wound about his arm and pulling open the shredded remains of his sleeve to reveal the wound. Parts of the cloth stuck to the wound, and she removed them as carefully as possible. An action she immediately regretted as it pulled at the scabs that had begun to form and started the bleeding anew. Thankfully, it was less than before.

She took the waterskin and ripped a strip of linen from her petticoat and then carefully cleaned the wound as best she could. He hissed through his teeth a few times but held still through her ministrations. Once it was clean, she ripped another strip from her petticoat and wound it carefully around his arm, tying it tight enough to keep pressure on the wound but not so tight that he wouldn't be able to use his arm.

"Try not to get wounded again. I'm running out of petticoat."

He laughed and rested his head against the wall. Rose gathered up the bloody cloths. "I, um…I never thanked you," she said.

William looked at her in surprise. "For what?"

"For saving my life."

He stared at her and then said, "Yes, well, I've heard the Lady Alice is quite demanding. I didna wish to be on the wrong end of her tongue should I have to inform her that her favorite maid had been killed on my watch."

Rose scowled, though her lips twitched with amusement.

"Besides which, I owe ye safe passage while ye're with me, since ye didna come with me willingly."

"Ah yes," she said softly. "I'll never forgive you for that, you know."

"Good. I deserve no forgiveness."

His voice was quiet, but harsh enough she flinched, though she knew it was not directed at her. Unsure of how to respond, she turned her attention back to his arm. She carefully cut the rest of his sleeve away. It was a shame to do, but the shirt was ruined in any case, and the fabric would be useful for further bandages. Perhaps she could add a new sleeve once they arrived at Kirkenroch if there was anything left of the shirt to salvage.

Finally, she said, "Well, owed or not, I thank you. I appreciate not being dead."

He laughed at that, and her stomach chose that inopportune moment to grumble loudly. His grin grew wider.

"Well I canna do much to make your accommodations more comfortable, but I can maybe do something about that."

He pushed away from the wall and went to the saddlebags. He rummaged through them before finally pulling out a few rock-hard oat cakes and handing one to her. She looked at it dubiously, and he chuckled again.

"It's no' so bad," he said. "Gnaw on it for a bit. It'll soften up."

"Actually, I might be able to do a bit better."

She went to her satchel and pulled out half a loaf of bread and two small apples that she had managed to grab from Ramsay's table.

"Verra nice," he said.

"Bread, apples, and bricks. That should keep us going until we reach Kirkenroch."

He laughed again and took a bite of his bread.

They ate in companionable silence for a few minutes, and her weariness again crept over her. She didn't want to sleep. She was afraid to close her eyes. Afraid when she opened them, enemies would be at their door. Or worse, they'd both fall asleep but William would never awake. His arm didn't look too bad, but she wasn't sure. She'd never dressed a knife wound before. It most likely needed to be stitched closed, but she had no sewing supplies with her. It would have to wait until they reached Kirkenroch. Which meant he needed to last until they got there.

"Tell me more about the Campbells and MacGregors," she said. "They don't get on well, it seems?"

William snorted. "That's an understatement, lass. Campbells and MacGregors dinna get along, over anything. They have fought for centuries over land, slights—imagined and otherwise—stolen women, damaged property. Any and every excuse. But," he said, leaning his head back against the wall again, "when the king ordered Malcolm to marry

Sorcha, the daughter of the Campbell chief, that forced a truce. Ramsay, of course, chose not to honor that and paid the price for his betrayal of his father and clan."

"And this is why he hates the MacGregors so passionately?" she asked.

"Aye. That and the fact that my kinsmen were responsible for the dismantling of his smuggling empire and theft of his betrothed. According to him. The Lady Elizabet insists she never would have wed the knave."

"Did Lady Elizabet really leave everything behind to wed a highwayman?"

"Aye. Quite against the highwayman's wishes, I might add."

Rose smiled. "It's quite romantic, I think."

"Aye, 'tis. But dinna tell Laird John I said so." William gave her a little half grin that sent her stomach flipping.

"Come," he said, throwing his apple core into the corner. "We can get a few hours rest before dawn. I dinna ken how ye feel, but I could use it."

Rose hadn't wanted to complain. After all, they were on the run for their lives and were trying to save their friends. Comforts like sleep didn't matter in such circumstances. But despite her fear, her body, at least, craved a few moments of rest.

He made her a small pallet in the corner using a blanket he pulled from one of the saddlebags. It certainly wasn't the most comfortable bed she had ever slept on, but she was warm and dry. And if she wished that a certain Highland rogue would lie by her side and keep her company, it was only because she'd grown used to his presence while she slept. And so she'd have something softer on which to pillow her head than the stone beneath her. Nothing more.

Liar!

• • •

William sat near the door, keeping watch while Rose slept, a gentle snore erupting from her every now and then. He tried to keep his thoughts on what they would do once they reached Kirkenroch, and away from the ever-present guilt that plagued him whenever he looked at Rose.

He couldn't do anything right. It was why he had jumped to volunteer when John and Philip had needed someone to spy on Ramsay. William had messed up everything he had tried to do, starting from the first job that he'd been given with his kinsmen. He'd ridden with John and his highwaymen crew. And he'd been arrogant and over-confident, despite it being his first time. He hadn't been in the saddle with them an hour when he'd accidentally shot Lady Elizabet.

And then, when he was supposed to be keeping guard while the men were watching Ramsay at the lady's estate, he had left his post to relieve himself, which allowed the Lady Elizabet to sneak past him. When he'd discovered her and tried to confront her, she'd nearly knocked him cold with a well-placed fist to his right cheek.

He was tired of feeling like a useless bumbling idiot around the highly trained warriors of the MacGregor clan. He had thought he'd finally found something he was good at. He could be the eyes and ears for the clan, watch Ramsay, become a trusted member of his gang, and warn his kinsmen when Ramsay finally decided to attack. Instead, he'd never fully gained Ramsay's trust, and then he'd gone and kidnapped an innocent maid. Which had not only ruined the plans Lady Alice had so carefully put into place but alerted Ramsay to Philip's whereabouts. And he'd brought Rose into danger. *And* through his actions, possibly led Ramsay straight to Laird John and his lady.

The only thing he could do that would make up for his

shortcomings was to get to Kirkenroch in time and warn everyone that Ramsay was on his way. Even still, he felt a failure because he hadn't been able to gather as much information as he needed to truly prepare his clansmen. Yes, they knew Ramsay was on the way, and he had some idea about the size of his crew and their provisions. But he couldn't truly know exact numbers or even an exact date because once again he had failed.

Just like he had exposed Rose to more danger. He did not regret killing Lionel. He'd been a dangerous man, and the act had removed one of Ramsay's most trusted lieutenants. More than that, the man had looked to assault Rose. William would have done much worse to him had she come to true harm.

As he would for any lady.

He sighed, knowing in his heart of hearts that his reaction had been spurred by the despair and terror he'd felt at seeing Lionel menacing Rose.

He watched the sky. They'd need to leave soon. The urgency to get back on the road grew. He must warn his kinsmen. But he couldn't bring himself to wake Rose yet. Shadows bruised the skin beneath her eyes, and she slept fitfully, her teeth chattering against the cold.

But at least she slept. He ached to lie beside her. To share his warmth, make her a little more comfortable. But he dared not let himself touch her. He tried to tell himself that the urge to wrap her in his arms was simply guilt from the situation in which he had put her. But even he didn't believe that.

Rose woke with a quiet gasp and sat upright, quickly glancing about the room.

"I'm here, lass," he said quietly and couldn't help the warmth that flowed through him when her shoulders sagged with relief at his voice.

She crawled over to him. "What are you doing?" she

asked. "I thought you were supposed to be resting."

"I am. But I must also keep watch."

"Will Ramsay come this direction?"

His heart clenched at the fear in her voice. "It's possible. But I wouldna think so. There are other, easier routes to Glenlyon, and he doesna ken the way to Kirkenroch or even that it exists. Plus, he'll be traveling with a large group. He willna wish to travel the main thoroughfares, but I can't imagine he would seek out such an out-of-the-way trail as this."

She nodded, and William sent up a quick prayer that he was right.

"But," she said, her forehead creased in thought, "he might not be traveling with such a large group. Remember the men who have been separating from us throughout the trip."

"Aye, ye're right," Will said, frowning.

"Oh! I never showed you!" She jumped up and went to her satchel, pulling out her apron.

"Ye wished to show me yer apron?" he asked with a laugh.

"Yes." She carefully unfolded it to reveal several smudges.

No…not smudges. He sat forward to get a closer look. X marks.

"What are these?" he asked.

"It's from the map in Ramsay's tent," she said, excitement in her voice. "I think this is Glenlyon." She pointed to the large X near the top. "And these could be where he's been sending the small groups of men. See how they surround the large X?"

"Aye. It could be." Excitement flooded him. Finally! Real information that might actually make a difference.

"You should get some sleep before we go," Rose said. "I can keep watch."

He shook his head. "I'll be all right. Get some more rest."

"I've rested."

He opened his mouth to argue again, and she held up her hand. "I've slept as much as I'm going to. If you are going to be stubborn and refuse to sleep, then we might as well be on our way."

He narrowed his eyes, trying to intimidate her into obeying him, though he knew that was a lost cause. She simply crossed her arms and stared at him.

"Fine. Have it yer way then."

She grinned and quickly gathered their things, once again taking care to store the apron in the satchel where it would be safe from the elements. She slung the satchel over her shoulder and put her hands in her pockets, only to jerk her head up in outraged shock.

"Damn you, William!"

He chuckled and ducked out of the doorway, her dagger safely in his waistband.

Chapter Ten

They rode up to the gates of Kirkenroch just after sunrise. A sleepy page ran to get his master and within a few minutes, they were met by John and Lady Elizabet.

"William," John said, clasping him in a quick hug. He took a step back, keeping his hands on William's shoulders to look him over. John frowned. "If ye're arriving at the break of dawn, bloodied and weary, I can guess yer news."

"Aye," William said. "Ramsay is on the march. And close."

John nodded and then turned at the sound of more feet clattering down the stairs.

"William?" Philip asked, hurrying toward them with Lady Alice.

She gasped and pulled Rose into a hug while Philip frowned. "What is wrong? What are ye doing here?"

"And why are you with him?" Alice added, looking at Rose.

John's grave face said more than William needed to. John was the jovial cousin, always quick to jest, always with a smile. With his dour expression, Philip knew instantly what was wrong.

"Ramsay," he said.

John nodded, and William put down the cup Elizabet had pressed into his hand. "He willna be far behind us. A day at the most. We rode as fast as we could but I wasna able to get away as quickly as I'd hoped. And with the horse carrying the both of us…"

Philip clapped his hand on Will's shoulder. "Ye did well, lad."

Will knew the *lad* was more a term of endearment than statement of his age, but he still cringed. His older cousins would probably always see him as the young lad they needed to protect.

"But how did the two of you come to be together?" Alice asked, frowning at Rose. "I left you on the docks at Dover. You were supposed to have returned to my parents."

"I'd planned to, my lady. But then—"

"I took her prisoner," Will said, knowing his tone suggested he'd been suffering for his actions ever since. But… he wasn't wrong. That didn't mean he hadn't enjoyed at least some of that suffering, but he didn't think it prudent to admit that to anyone.

"You did *what*?" Alice asked, taking a threatening step closer.

"It was a misunderstanding—" he started before Rose cut in.

"Because you jumped to conclusions and rather than wait two minutes for me to explain, you trussed me up and hauled me off for questioning. Thinking I was a spy for Ramsay!"

"What?" Alice gasped.

William sighed. They'd been getting along so well. That whole kidnapping thing would be biting him in the arse until the day he died. "Oh, for the thousandth time, woman, I'm sorry. Ye have no idea how sorry. It was the worst mistake I've ever made in my entire life. And ye've been making me pay for it for weeks now."

"As well you should be! Just because you were off playing spy doesn't mean the rest of us weren't simply trying to mind our own business. And then you had to drag me into all of this, when I had strict orders from my lady—"

"Must we go over all this again?" William said, rubbing his face. "At this point, madam, I'd sell my soul to the devil himself if it meant I could undo what I did, but I cannae do that, so ye're either going to have to learn to forgive me or get on with killing me, because I'd rather die a swift death by yer blade than listen to ye naggin' me about it for the rest of my life."

"I'd be glad to oblige, but you took my dagger!"

"Then I'll gladly give ye my own!"

"That's not what you said a few hours ago when I tried to take it from you."

William opened his mouth to respond, but Philip put himself between them. "Now, I'm sure that's a fascinating story, but as long as the lass hasna been hurt in any way…" He looked at Rose with a cocked eyebrow, and she begrudgingly shook her head, even as her eyes narrowed at Will.

Philip nodded. "Well then, I say we let the matter drop and send these two to rest and refresh themselves. They've had an arduous journey in order to bring us this news. We need to use it to our advantage. All else can wait until after Ramsay has been dealt with."

Alice didn't look like she wanted to let the matter drop, but even she couldn't argue with the need to fortify themselves against the coming attack.

She bundled up Rose and took her upstairs, though Rose looked like she was about to argue. Will knew she'd much rather be with the men discussing the coming attack.

He gave her a little smile and wave as Alice dragged her up the stairs. Her expression promised retaliation for that bit of childishness, and he grinned.

He turned back to Philip and John, who were both looking at him with confused but amused expressions. Then John chuckled and clapped a hand on his shoulder.

"Come, Will. Let's away to the kitchens and get some food in ye while ye fill us in on the finer details."

They sat around the table near the kitchen hearth while Will ate some cold roast chicken and crusty bread.

"I truly am that sorry about the lass, Philip, I swear it…" he said, his amusement over riling Rose fading in the face of his cousins' certain disapproval.

"Pay it no mind, Will. For now, anyway. There's more important matters to discuss."

Will nodded and took another bracing drink of ale.

John pulled up a stool and sat down. "I'd love to ken how the maid plays into all this, but for now," he said, holding his hand up against the immediate defensiveness Will felt, "tell us the relevant information on Ramsay. How far away is he? How many men with him? Do ye ken what he is planning?"

Will told them all he knew, from the moment he'd left Philip at the docks, to when he'd rejoined Ramsay's men in his disguise as one of them, to the moment he and Rose had broken away.

Philip and John listened with growing concern.

"We havena much time then," Philip said.

"Nay, my laird," Will said. "A day or two at most. Perhaps less if he's discovered my deception."

John called a lad in and sent him scurrying off to Glenlyon as fast as he could go. Then he turned back to them. "Thank ye, Will," John said, clapping both hands on his shoulders. "Ye've given us a chance to prepare a defense. One we didna have last time. Let's not waste it!"

"I do have a bit more information," Will said. He grabbed Rose's satchel from under his chair and pulled out her apron.

"A lassie's dirty apron?" Philip said with a frown.

"Rose's apron, to be exact. But not dirty."

He laid it flat on the table and pointed out the X marks. "I canna be sure the large X is Glenlyon, but it stands to reason, as Ramsay doesna ken about Kirkenroch. As far as I was able to discover."

"We can hope. But it's a good assumption," John said. "And these marks?" He pointed to the smaller ones.

"All along the journey, small groups of men broke away from the larger group and went off alone. At first I assumed that they were deserting. But their disappearance never flustered Ramsay and it happened in regular enough intervals that it must have been intentional. Rose and I believe these smaller X marks note where each of these groups of men will be stationed."

John and Philip exchanged a glance at Will's mention of Rose but didn't say anything. Instead, Philip nodded. "It's a good strategy, damn the man. Surrounds Glenlyon neatly, leaving only the loch side without groups of men."

"True. Though they'd be hard put to sneak up on us from that direction," John said.

"Aye," Philip agreed. "And if this is Kirkenroch, then it leaves only the cliffside open. Again, a side which would be nearly impossible to penetrate, regardless."

They all nodded and stared at the Xs. Then John turned to Will. "If ye had to guess, what would you think the large X denotes?"

Anxiety wormed its way through Will's chest. If he guessed wrong, it could be the difference between winning or losing this battle. Between lives lost and lives saved. He hesitated to say anything, but both men waited.

"I canna be sure. But I believe it is Glenlyon. As far as I

ken, Ramsay is focused on Glenlyon, as he has always been. He's never mentioned any destination but Glenlyon. And as ye've pointed out, few ken the existence of Kirkenroch. Those who remember it think it's still a ruin."

Both men nodded in agreement. "I think ye're right, lad," John said, his lips twitching a bit at Will's obvious irritation at being called lad.

"Dinna take it to heart, Will," Philip said with a wry smile. "Ye could be as shriveled and gray as Malcolm's old cat and he'd still call ye *lad*."

John grinned. "He's not wrong."

Will groaned and carefully refolded the apron. He found a bit of cloth and twine and wrapped it up before calling in another stable boy to run it to Glenlyon. He relayed the information about the Xs, making the lad repeat it to him before letting him go.

"Well," John said. "We've done what we can to warn Malcolm. Now let's do what we can to fortify Kirkenroch. We may not have much time, and the day isna getting younger."

Will nodded. "What do ye need me to do?"

They discussed strategies for the coming battle with contingency plans depending on where Ramsay attacked. Will was pleased they treated him as an equal, giving him real responsibilities. Whether Ramsay attacked at Glenlyon or Kirkenroch, Will would stay with the men at Kirkenroch. A small part of him chaffed at not being given the chance to go to Glenlyon and fight Ramsay. But the women would be staying behind at Kirkenroch. Will knew how much his kinsmen cared for their wives. To be asked to protect them was a great honor and responsibility, and Will was humbled at his cousins' trust in him.

And Rose would stay behind with her lady. Which meant he could keep an eye on her as well. Whether she wanted him to or not.

"All right. We canna do more tonight," Philip said. Then he put a hand on Will's shoulder. "We need ye to get some rest."

Will batted his hand out of the way. "Despite yer jests, I'm no' some stable boy who needs coddling."

"Aye, man, we ken that well," Philip said. "But ye've also spent the night riding like the devil was on yer arse to get here. With a cantankerous lassie and a bleeding wound to boot. Ye'll be no good to us if ye canna hold a sword."

The fact that Rose had said nearly the same thing to him made it all the more galling. Even more so because he knew they weren't wrong.

"Get yer arm looked at. It may need stitching if it's still seeping like that," he said, pointing to the growing red spot on the bandage. "And then get a few hours of sleep. There's a room at the end of the hall that should do. Meet me back in the courtyard after the midday meal and I'll put ye to work."

Will wanted to argue again but John frowned. Will sighed. "Aye, my laird."

"Good. And Will," he said, before Will could leave the room.

"Aye?"

"If ye want to visit yer lassie, my Bess put her in the small chamber off my suite," John said with a grin. "Second floor, third door on the right."

Will left the room, cursing under his breath as his cousins laughed at his expense. Bastards.

Yet, when he'd climbed the staircase, instead of going to the room at the end of the hallway, he turned to the third door on the right.

He had to be out of his mind. But he raised his hand to knock anyway.

• • •

Rose opened the door, eyes widening a bit upon seeing William standing there.

His rather sheepish grin had her lips twitching in response. "Now that ye have some sewing supplies at yer disposal, I thought perhaps ye could tend to my arm."

She opened her mouth to point out there were more qualified women at the manor to tend him. But instead, she opened the door wider and stepped aside so he could enter.

He came in and looked about her room. It was small but comfortable. A soft cot piled with blankets took up one end of the room, and a fire crackled warmly in the hearth. She even had a narrow, paned window with a cushioned seat along with a table and two chairs. Her room was not hung with the rich tapestries and paintings that were displayed in the larger rooms, but that was as it should be. She was happy with her quarters. Even more so because her mistress was right next door.

"Sit down," she bade him.

He did so, unwinding his kilt from his shoulders.

There was a bit of blood crusting the bandage, but not nearly as bad as before. Still, once she unwound the bandage and got a good look at the wound, there were several gaps that would heal better with a stitch or two.

She poured a bit of water from the pitcher on her table and rummaged through the sewing basket she'd found near the bed. In addition to the needles and thread, she also found several clean strips of linen. She snorted softly. Maybe they were used to stitching up their men as often as their socks in the Highlands. It didn't surprise her. Most tales she'd heard of Scots made them sound like savages who were constantly warring with one another. And the stories William had told her, along with what she'd seen on their travels, hadn't done much to change that notion. All the more reason to get back home to England as soon as possible.

She cleaned the wound as best she could and threaded a needle. But she paused before she began. He glanced up at her, a question in his eyes.

"Are you sure you want me to do this?" she asked. "I've never stitched flesh before."

He gave her that half grin she loved so much and shrugged. "It's much the same as stitching cloth. Mayhap a bit tougher to get through."

She raised her eyebrows. "Stitched yourself up before, have you?"

"Aye. A time or two."

She snorted and leaned back over him. "I'll try not to hurt you."

"Och, it'll be fine…" His voice broke off with a hiss when she made her first jab. She bit her lip.

"One second," he said, reaching over to where she'd laid his coat to dig out a small flask of whisky. He downed three large gulps, then nodded at her to continue.

He flinched when she poked the needle through the other side of the wound and gently pulled the two sides together. But he didn't protest, so she kept going, putting in two or three stitches, then biting off the thread and moving to another gaping spot.

William sat silently through her ministrations, taking another drink now and then, his eyes watching her. Every now and then she'd raise her gaze to meet his and looked away each time, her cheeks growing warmer.

Finally, she finished. She stepped back with a sigh and regarded her handiwork. "It's not too bad," she said, her brow creased in a frown.

He looked down. "Verra fine," he said, glancing back at her.

She flushed again and got a clean strip of linen to wrap around his arm. "I hope it won't hamper you too much if there's fighting to be done."

He snorted. "I've fought with worse."

"I bet you have," she said.

He stood and dragged his coat back over his shoulder. She stepped back, expecting him to leave now that she'd done what he'd asked. He did move to the door, but instead of leaving, he remained standing in front of it, his back to her.

She crossed her arms and waited.

"I am...sorry, that I took ye," he said finally, his gravelly voice so low she almost couldn't hear it. "I dinna ken if I've said that to ye yet." He turned back to her and gave her a small smile. "And meant it, at least."

She smiled at that, her heart thumping happily. "I suppose you want me to forgive you all your sins in case the battle goes poorly," she said, trying to joke, though her words were anything but funny.

His smile faded. "No. There's no forgiveness for what I've done."

She frowned, her mouth opening to argue, but he held up a hand.

"Dinna argue, lass. Not this time. Nothing you can say will absolve me. I took ye, an innocent, put ye in harm's way in the lair of the very devil. And in doing so, brought that devil to the doorstep of those I hold most dear. How can I expect forgiveness for that?"

"William," she murmured, her heart breaking for him.

He stood, tall and proud before her, but the haunted eyes that stared into hers betrayed the regret that tormented his very soul.

"You may not be asking for it, and you may not accept it. But you do have my forgiveness."

He closed his eyes and shook his head, and she took his face in both her hands, forcing him to look at her.

"You made a mistake. Not one I enjoyed, I'll grant you

that," she said with a smile that drew a small smile from him. "But you're as human as the rest of us. No one is infallible, Will. And you've since saved my life—more than once."

"Yer life was in danger only because of the mistake I made," he said shaking his head. "It doesna atone for what I did."

"You can't know that," she insisted. He shook his head, but she pressed on. "I mean it. You don't know what would have happened had you not taken me. I wasn't happy letting my mistress board that ship. I would have returned home because I promised her I would. But I'd already started thinking of plans to follow her. I might have done something even more stupid had you not intervened. Or I might have been taken anyway. Lionel saw me that day. He might have seen me return home and decided to take me at some point. Either way, my mistress's secret would have been discovered, and I'd have been in more danger had I followed her on my own. And as it stands, I am here at my mistress's side, where I belong. And I'm not alone."

She forced herself to keep her gaze locked with his, even if the words she'd uttered, and their implications, made her want to turn and run. He stared into her eyes for what felt like forever. Then he brushed a thumb across her cheek.

"I dinna deserve yer forgiveness."

"You have it anyway."

His lips twitched. "Must ye argue with everything I say?"

"Yes," she said without hesitation.

He laughed and then sighed deeply and dropped his hand. "I should let ye rest."

She shook her head. "I've rested enough. I couldn't sleep now."

"Nothing I say will change yer mind, will it?"

She smiled up at him. "No."

He sighed. "Ye'd test the patience of the saints

themselves."

"Thank you," she said.

He laughed and shook his head. Then he rubbed his hand over his face. Despite his insistence, she could see how weary he was.

"Truce?" she asked. "For tonight, at least?"

He chuckled again. "Truce."

"Good. Come." She took his hand and drew him to the cushioned seat below the window and drew him down so that he sat beside her.

He turned, his back against the wall so he could gaze out the window, and she followed, leaning back against him. He wrapped his arms around her and held her close. She closed her eyes, knowing he couldn't see her face, and savored the feel of his arms about her. Their truce wouldn't last. He'd always annoy her. He'd probably never forgive himself for all his perceived sins, no matter what she said, and that would be a problem. He was a stubborn Scot who belonged in his savage Highlands, and she was an English maid who belonged...well, she no longer knew where she belonged.

At Lady Alice's side, she supposed. Wherever that ended up being. She longed with all her heart to return home. To a civilized city far from the terrifying clan feuds that apparently still raged in the Scottish wilds. To the familiar house where she'd grown up. To her grandmother and the bevy of servants in the Chivers' household who were more like her family than her real kin.

But for one night, she could let him hold her. Let herself feel how it might be if things were different. If they were different.

There was still a good chance one or both of them wouldn't survive the fight that was coming. She spoke of forgiveness now, but he wasn't wrong. His actions had put them all in grave danger. He'd done much to make up for that mistake. Hopefully, it would be enough. But if her lady were to be harmed…if she herself came to harm…

No, it wasn't all William's fault. The true villain was the man who hunted them. But Rose couldn't guarantee that her feelings wouldn't change if the fight were to go against them.

But for this moment in time, she would pretend nothing else in the world existed except the two of them.

Behind her, William's breathing grew deep and even, and the arms about her loosened, although even in his sleep he kept them about her. She smiled and wrapped her arms about his.

It would work out. They'd defeat their enemies. The alternative was too painful to consider.

Chapter Eleven

Toward dawn, they spotted a lone rider in the distance, galloping like hell itself was on his tail.

They were already dressed. They went downstairs, right behind Philip and Lady Alice. John and Lady Elizabet were already in the Great Hall, preparing themselves and sending others scurrying.

"He's here," Philip said, not making it a question. John nodded. "Spotted a few miles away with a large group of men. He marches on Malcolm."

The tight knot of anxiety that had lodged itself in Will's gut loosened. He feared for those at Glenlyon, but it had been his call on where Ramsay would attack, and the thought he might have been wrong had been a heavy burden.

What men were at the manor were already scurrying to and fro, preparing to ride out.

"He attacks Glenlyon?" Philip asked, eyes wide with surprise. "He's a reckless lunatic, but I never believed he'd be so mad as to attack The Lion in his own lair."

John strapped his sword to his hip. "Aye, well I wouldna

be surprised by anything that bastard did." He looked at Philip and then Will. "But it ends today."

They both nodded and then Philip and John turned to their wives to discuss the arrangements for the coming battle. Will already knew his place. He'd stay at Kirkenroch and help lead the men so that Philip could ride to Glenlyon with a small contingent of men and help Malcolm. John would not leave his heavily pregnant wife.

Both Lady Elizabet and Lady Alice seemed to find their men's insistence that they remain in hiding irksome. Their men had their hands full getting them to agree. Especially Philip with Lady Alice. But after a few minutes of arguing, she finally seemed to agree to stay put.

Will caught Rose's gaze and gave her half a smile. She returned it and then turned back to her task. She and Will were in charge of overseeing moving what women and children were in the house up to a small, hidden storage chamber off Lady Alice's suite, along with securing provisions to keep them comfortable, while John mobilized the men who'd stayed behind.

Of course, Rose had her own ideas on how this would best be accomplished.

Will moved through the kitchens, setting women to gathering up food and drink for those who would be in hiding. Rose followed close on his heels. As they had no idea how long such tactics might be necessary, he debated how much to gather along with which items would be most useful. And Rose disagreed with him on almost every choice.

"Not those," Rose said after he pointed to a bushel of apples.

Will closed his eyes and sighed. "What is wrong with apples? They are juicy and will give the children something to suck on if the attack lasts long enough that drink grows scarce."

"And gnawing on those will make small stomachs upset, especially those small green ones, and especially if there is little else in their bellies. You don't want a room full of sick children do you? The smell alone would lead the enemy right to us."

He clenched his jaw, then nodded. "Fine. Take half as many." He raised a hand to point at several loaves of bread but Rose was already shaking her head.

"Ye canna be objecting to bread," he said, ready to pull his hair out by the root.

"Not entirely, but the travel rations will give the younger children something to gnaw on."

"I thought we didna want them gnawing on anything."

"We don't want them gnawing on green apples. Oat loaves are fine."

He plastered a strained smile on his lips. "How about ye take care of matters here, and I'll do a walk-through of the rooms on this floor to be sure everyone is where they should be."

He turned and tried to leave before Rose could follow him. Another hour of her hounding his heels and berating him for every decision he made and the temptation was strong to turn her over to the enemy.

She quickly pointed out a few things to the housekeeper and hurried to follow.

He strode by two rooms, poking his head in before moving on, when she caught up with him.

"You can't check the rooms like that! You have to actually go inside."

He rounded on her, startling her enough that she jumped and pressed back against the wall. He took advantage, looming over her so she was pinned.

"Do ye doubt my ability to carry out the orders my laird set out for me?" he asked, leaning in so he could speak quietly.

Not that there was anyone to hear. Despite her worries, everyone save he, Rose, and the housekeeper had long since taken position where they were bid.

She blinked up at him, her eyes wide with surprise. "No, of course not."

"Then why are ye questioning every decision I make?"

"I'm not, I'm merely..."

He cocked an eyebrow, and she jutted her chin in the air, standing her ground for a second before her shoulders slumped in defeat.

"I am merely trying to make sure that everything goes to plan. That I'm doing everything I can to help. I feel responsible..."

Will shook his head and took her chin in his fingers. "If anyone is responsible, it's me. As ye've told me repeatedly," he said, smiling to lessen the accusation. "And ye werena wrong. As much as it pains me to hear it. Over and over again."

Her cheeks flushed. "I suppose I could mention it a little less."

"Perish the thought," he said, releasing her chin. "However, I would appreciate a little more confidence in my ability to carry out my orders."

She released a long sigh and nodded. "But Will, I can't sit about doing nothing while the men prepare for war. I must do something."

"I dinna object to ye accompanying me. I merely object to yer objections."

She laughed at that. "I shall try to keep them to myself."

It wasn't much of a promise, but it was likely the best he'd get. He leaned in farther, slowly enough she could move if she wished. Instead, she tilted her face up, kissing him back when his lips brushed against hers.

"When this is all over, we need to discuss a few things," he said.

"Yes," she said, staring up into his eyes. "We do."

He stepped back, releasing her, and they went on about their tasks. She even managed to keep from questioning his every move. For the most part.

Finally, everything was done, and there was nothing left to do but wait for the attack.

Alice and Philip's chamber had a small storage room behind it that had only one small window set high in the wall and was cleverly disguised behind a tapestry. The women and children were ushered in there and hidden away.

When John tried to get Elizabet to go inside, however, he ran into some resistance.

Alice and Rose exchanged a glance and turned to hide their smiles as John argued with his stubborn wife, but Will scowled.

"What is it about women that makes them argue over even the most reasonable request?" he said, not really directing the comment at anyone. But Rose, naturally, chose to answer.

"Perhaps men don't always know as much as they think they do. Women do know best sometimes, especially when it comes to what they are capable of."

Will snorted. And then ducked to dodge the wadded roll of bandages Rose chucked at his head.

John seemed to be wavering on whether or not he should guard the main doors with his men or stay in the hidden chamber with his wife. Lady Elizabet was dangerously close to giving birth, and Will could understand his laird's reluctance at leaving her. He itched to get out there and fight. He wanted nothing more than to rout Ramsay and his men, remove them from the face of the earth so they could no longer threaten those he cared for. But watching the struggle on John's face as he tried to reconcile his duties as laird with his love for his wife struck Will anew, and he stepped forward.

"I'll stay and watch over them, my lord," William offered.

"Should we come under attack, I'll make sure they are well hidden before any danger descends."

John hesitated but finally nodded. "Thank you, Will. I'll rest easier with ye here to protect her." He still looked worried, but some of the tension had eased from his face. He turned back to his wife, murmuring to her before giving her a quick kiss.

The ladies sat on the bed, Elizabet rubbing her swollen belly while Alice fussed over her. Rose came back to his side.

"That was very gallant of you," she said. He raised an eyebrow at her, and she rolled her eyes. "What? I can pay a compliment when it's deserved."

He chuckled. "Aye? I suppose miracles do happen every now and then."

She scowled. "Don't make me take it back."

He laughed again, and her face softened. She looked back at the women on the bed. "I meant it," she said quietly. "I know how much you'd like to be out in the thick of the fighting. How much it cost you to offer to stay behind."

His gaze took in the ladies before him and then shifted to the one at his side. "No' such a great cost as all that to protect what is most precious."

Her gaze shot to his in surprise and he cleared his throat, stepping away from her. "I must make sure we are secure here," he said, bowing his head before moving away.

He hadn't meant to say anything to her and could only hope he hadn't betrayed too much. But Rose's eyes followed him as he patrolled, checking doors, looking out the windows, guarding the entrance. They would have to resolve whatever this was between them. Once Ramsay had been taken care of. If they all survived.

The sun climbed higher in the sky, but no word came from Glenlyon. Surely they should have heard something by now.

His charges were mostly quiet, and he even had a small respite from Rose's focused attention when she went into the hidden room to help one of the women settle her new baby. But a sudden curse from Lady Elizabet drew his gaze from his post by the window.

She was brushing at a wet spot on the front of her gown. "I'm afraid I'm growing clumsier by the day," she said. She hauled herself out of her chair with a sigh. "I'm going to change."

William frowned. "My laird said that no one was to leave this chamber, my lady."

"I am going only to the end of the hall. It'll be a quick moment."

William glanced back and forth between Elizabet's retreating back and the hidden door behind the tapestry. He'd been charged with protecting both, something that Elizabet was making impossible. He focused his gaze on Alice, trying to make it clear he wanted her to side with him and get Elizabet back into the dressing room. He didn't want to upset the lady, but he'd promised to protect her. John would never forgive him if something happened to her. And he'd never forgive himself for failing his kinsman.

Alice wavered, clearly thinking the same thing he was. But her gaze softened when she looked at Elizabet, and he realized she'd made the wrong choice.

"I'll go with her," Alice said. "I'll make sure she hurries."

William's frown darkened at that. "Forgive me, my lady, but both of ye should be in with the other women. I really must insist…"

But Elizabet was already out of the door, muttering about being uncomfortable enough without being wet, too.

"I'll look after her," Alice promised, following her friend. "We'll make haste."

William paced the room, going from the window to the

doorway, back and forth. Dread settled in his gut. Something was about to happen. And the two ladies he'd been charged to protect had escaped him. He cursed under his breath, poking his head out the chamber doorway one more time. He could hear them rustling about in the chamber a few doors down. Hopefully, they were nearly finished.

He paced back to the window and glanced outside briefly. Then he turned and pressed close to the glass, his heart hammering. Was that movement in the courtyard?

The thick glass of the window made it difficult to see, but as he watched, a large group of men poured through the courtyard, fighting their way through those stationed outside.

Ramsay! It must be. He'd been wrong. He'd sent everyone to Glenlyon! Guilt and terror shot through him but he jumped to action.

"We're under attack!" he said.

Rose darted from the hidden room, the bandages she'd been rolling tumbling from her fingers.

"Get them inside," he said, gesturing to the few women who'd been milling about the room.

They were already scurrying to do his bidding and get themselves hidden in the secret chamber. He had to get to the ladies, Elizabet and Alice.

Rose slammed the secret chamber door behind her and stood in front of it. He wanted to argue with her, insist that she hide away as well. But he knew she wouldn't listen, and they were out of time.

He hauled her to him and pressed a fast, hard kiss to her lips. "We have much to discuss when this is all done, ye stubborn wee madwoman. But for now..."

He pulled the extra sword he'd strapped to his hip that morning from its scabbard. "Take this. Yer wee dagger is in yer pocket, but should ye need something more..." He handed her the sword.

She stared at him, eyes wide and mouth open, but she didn't argue. For once.

Shouts and metal clashing with metal rang through the house.

"She's here, my lord!" a man shouted in the hallway.

Will sprinted for the doorway, just in time to intercept two men who were charging for Alice and Elizabet, who stood frozen outside the far chamber door.

He shouted and swung his sword, catching them by surprise. His blade slashed through the man nearest him, and he fell to the floor, his dead eyes staring wide.

The other man swung his sword and Will narrowly dodged it. Their blades clashed as they both swung again. There was no way to get the ladies into the hidden chamber now, not with them fighting right in front of the door and more men coming up the stairs.

He ducked to avoid another thrust and then spun. His gaze briefly met Rose's. She stood in the doorway, a large vase in her hands.

"Duck!" she warned.

He didn't hesitate. The vase sailed out of the chamber's doorway, crashing into William's opponent and distracting him long enough for William to turn and look at Alice and Elizabet. He shouted one word.

"Run!"

. . .

Rose paused only long enough to make sure William was unharmed. He turned to the ladies in the hall and shouted at them to run. Which meant he intended to stay behind and guard their escape.

Terror for him flooded through her, but she wouldn't let his sacrifice be in vain. She flew out the door, Will's sword in her hand and a prayer in her heart that he'd survive.

She ran for the women who stood rooted with fear at the end of the hallway.

"We need to go, my lady," she said to Lady Alice. "Now!"

She thrust her dagger into Alice's hand, her heart clenching at the sight of it. Will must have slipped it into her pocket again that morning. The thought that she'd never again be able to steal it back from him after he'd stolen it from her made her want to howl at the heavens. Instead, she looped an arm around Elizabet's waist and half hauled her to the stairs.

They led to the old kitchens and a quick glance around didn't offer any hope of adequate concealment. More shouts and clashing steel spurred them out the door. They stayed plastered to the wall of the house while they took a second to gauge their surroundings. It sounded like the main bulk of the fighting had moved inside, which might give them a chance to hide themselves in the woods.

Rose tried to remember the location of all those small *X*s on the map. The last thing she wanted to do was lead her ladies right into a group of Ramsay's men. But she wasn't familiar with Kirkenroch. She couldn't be sure where those *X*s might be in relation to the actual land. And with the sound of clashing swords and shouts and running feet growing closer, they didn't have many options. They couldn't go back into the manor. They'd have to take their chances in the woods.

"This way!" she said. She and Alice half supported, half dragged Elizabet into the small copse of woods at the back of the manor.

They hadn't gone far when the unmistakable sound of running footsteps came from behind them.

"We must hide her," Alice said, frantic in her need to find a place to hide Elizabet. "We can't outrun whoever is coming. Not with…"

She didn't need to finish her sentence. They couldn't go far with Elizabet in her condition. Even now, she bent over her belly, her face twisted in pain.

The pounding footsteps came closer. More than one set. Terror set Rose's heart to pounding so hard her head swam, but she fought it back.

"There!" Alice said, pointing to a bramble of bushes and ferns where they could maybe hide Elizabet.

But it was already too late.

Three men entered the clearing. Led by the one they all feared the most.

Elizabet's face lost what little color had been left. "Ramsay," she gasped.

The devil himself had found them. He narrowed in on Elizabet, the cruelty and hatred emanating from him twisting his face into the visage of a demon.

Rose raised her sword, intending to swing it at him, but one of his men stepped in front of her before she could.

"I wouldn't do that, poppet," he said. "The master's come all this way to have a word with the lady. You wouldn't want to deny him that, would you?"

She glared at him but stood down. He leered at her but as long as she wasn't attacking, he seemed content to let her be. But she had no delusions that he would remain so. He seemed to be waiting for orders from Ramsay, who was busy spewing his hate-filled rhetoric at Elizabet and Alice. And whatever he was saying made them both go pale.

Rose stepped closer to Elizabet, trying to give her whatever comfort and support she could.

"Where is John?" Elizabet asked Ramsay, her voice strained.

Ramsay raised a brow. "The last I saw your paramour, he was bleeding on the floor of this ruin you've been living in."

Elizabet swayed against Rose, who wrapped one

arm about her, supporting her as best she could while still maintaining a tight grip on her sword. John had fallen. Had Will?

She fought back the black wave of despair that threatened to overtake her. She had to protect her ladies.

"His mistake was in staying here and not riding to Glenlyon like the rest," Ramsay said, clearly relishing Elizabet's pain. "I knew he'd never leave your side. One of the stable boys was most forthcoming about where he was likely to be. Of course, I slit his throat anyway. Wouldn't do to reward such disloyalty."

"You evil bastard," Alice said. Rose heartily agreed.

"Now, now," he said, his tone placating, though his face had gone a strange mottled shade of red. "Such language doesn't become a lady." Then he waved his hand. "Enough of this. Take care of those two," he said to his men. "Try not to damage Lady Alice too much. But leave the Lady Elizabet. She's mine to punish."

Elizabet put a hand on Alice's arm but dropped it when another pain gripped her. Rose struggled to support her and still grip the sword. She would need both hands to swing it, if it came to that. And she knew it would. They were far from the house and, with the fighting going on, she doubted anyone would even hear their screams. If there were anyone left.

The men advanced, smiling, obviously seeing no threat. Well, they were going to get a surprise. From the corner of her eye, she could see Alice straighten up, her face still pale but determined, her hand tightly gripping the dagger Rose had given her. Good. Pride for her mistress strengthened her own courage. They were probably going to lose this fight, but they could do some damage first.

One of the men lunged at Alice, and she slashed out at him, yelling for all she was worth. Rose grinned and let out a bloodcurdling scream. The man bearing down on her hesitated, startled at her outburst. She jumped at his distraction and swung her sword for all she was worth.

It sliced into his leg, deep enough to glance off bone if the reverberation that jolted up her arms was any indication.

He screamed in pain and rage and swiped at her with his own sword, but his efforts were hampered by the blood pouring from his leg. Still, the weight of the sword in her own hands was already too much for her. The tip dragged along the ground as her assailant backed her up against a tree. She still managed to keep him at bay by hefting the sword and swinging it every time he ventured too near. But she wouldn't be able to maintain it for long. She'd be dead already if she hadn't managed to bloody him in that first attack.

Rose quickly glanced around her, praying for help. Ramsay stalked Elizabet. By the look on his face, he was enjoying drawing it out, relishing the rising terror in his victim. Alice was on the ground. Her attacker lashed out, punching her with his fist. Rose gasped and shouted, swinging her sword again, though her muscles screamed and trembled. She had to get to Alice before the man atop her killed her.

The sound of a shot ringing through the clearing froze everyone.

Elizabet stood pressed against a tree, a pistol in each hand. She'd obviously fired one, as a faint puff of smoke dissipated from its muzzle. She dropped it as Ramsay clutched his side and staggered away from her, spewing rage-filled profanity. She fired again and this time, the bullet found its mark, square in Ramsay's chest. He sank to his knees and then toppled to the ground.

Elizabet dropped the gun and slumped against the tree at her back.

Rose smiled and redoubled her grip on her sword. She swung. Her attacker, his gaze still focused on his fallen master, didn't react in time, and the blade sliced across his belly.

But it wasn't deep enough. It seemed to only enrage him. He struck out, his fist connecting with her chin. She dropped to her knees, her ears ringing from the blow. Black spots ate at her vision and she fought against them.

There was a pounding noise coming from somewhere. She put her hand up to her head, but the sound grew louder. Her attacker froze, then staggered on his wounded leg. Hands reached out to pull him away from her.

"Will?" she asked, her voice faint even to her own ears.

It wasn't Will's face that peered into her own. But it seemed friendly enough. She glanced to the side to see Elizabet cradled in someone's arms, but she couldn't see who it was. The black clouds grew stronger, and she finally couldn't fight them anymore.

Her sword dropped from fingers she could no longer feel, and the world went black.

Chapter Twelve

Several minutes earlier...

With more men thundering up the hall stairs, Will had only a second to meet Rose's gaze. The man she'd hit with the vase shook his head. He'd be on his feet again soon. And the others would be upon him in moments. Rose's eyes grew bright, as if with unshed tears. Then she jutted that stubborn chin of hers in the air and gave him a tiny nod. With a shout, she gathered up her ladies and led them out of the hallway toward a back staircase.

"That was a dirty trick," the man who'd been hit said as he got to his feet.

Will dragged his gaze back to his opponent and smiled. "If ye wanted a fair fight, ye shouldna ha' attacked a house full o' women and children."

He hefted his sword and stood ready to swing. The man before him shrugged. "I go where my master tells me. I'm not paid to ask questions."

"With a master like Ramsay, I'm surprised ye're paid at

all."

Three more men rounded the corner and stopped short at the sight of Will. He recognized two of them. And they obviously recognized him, judging from their confused frowns.

"Butler?" one of them—Thomas, if he remembered correctly—said. "What the devil are you doing here? Last I heard, you'd deserted from camp. And why are you fighting with Murphy?"

Will shrugged, but his heart hammered against his ribs. "I merely wished a quick visit home. And here ye are battering down my door. If ye wished me to return, ye only had to ask."

Thomas frowned again, but at least they weren't attacking. Yet. Will needed to stall them long enough for Rose and the ladies to get to safety. He'd never win against so many, but perhaps some sense of comradery or at least confusion would give him a chance to escape. The women and children hidden in Lady Alice's chamber should be safe enough as long as they remained in hiding. He wanted to plant himself in front of the door and fight any who tried to enter. But that would only alert their enemies that there was something inside worth protecting.

No, he needed to lead them away.

He slowly backed up, one step at a time, keeping his gaze on the men in front of him. Thomas's sword dropped a bit, but they were still on guard. They were, however, keeping pace with him, slowly stalking him down the hallway.

"I'm no' yer enemy," he said, his gaze flicking to two more men who joined them. "There's no reason for us to be fighting one another."

Murphy snorted and rubbed his head. "Not my enemy, eh? You killed George," he said, jerking his head toward the body they'd all ignored until then. "And someone hit me over the head."

Will shrugged again, pretending a nonchalance he didn't feel. "A reflex. It wasna I who attacked first. I merely attempted to defend myself and my home."

"This is your home?" Thomas asked. "Why would you be working for Ramsay if you had a place like this?"

One of the men in the back looked into Lady Alice's chamber, and Will's heart lurched. He needed to get them all out of the hallway and out of the house. He didn't want to take the same route that Rose had taken, but there was no way he could get past the gang in the hallway to go down the other stairs. He could go into one of the other chambers, but there would be no escape from there. Even if he managed to get out a window, he doubted anyone would follow him.

He hesitated a second more and then decided. He'd have to put his trust in Rose and have faith that she'd gotten the ladies out of the house. Or at least hidden safely. Because if he didn't act quickly, the group in front of him might decide to start exploring. The hallway was too narrow for them all to fight him up there. But if he ran, they might all follow.

"I never said this was mine. Only that it was my home."

Thomas's frown deepened and Will backed up more, quickening his pace ever so slightly. He was nearly to the stairwell now. He needed a slight head start, of course, but he couldn't get too far ahead. They needed to follow him.

"As for why I'd work for Ramsay, well, that is easy to answer." He took a deep breath and then smiled. "My name is no' Butler. It's Will MacGregor, at yer service," he said with a little bow. "I was sent to Ramsay's camp to spy on the evil bastard. Did a fair job of it, too, I reckon."

"Why, you traitorous swine," Thomas said, lunging for him.

Will didn't wait to see if the rest were as offended as Thomas. He just turned and sprinted for the stairwell, pulling over the iron sconce that stood in front of it as he did so. That would slow them down. A little. His wounded arm burned with pain, and a warm stickiness trickled under his sleeve. The stitches had most likely broken open, but he couldn't worry about it then. He ran down the stairs as fast as he could. From the clattering behind him, he was definitely being followed. He could only hope no one decided to stay behind.

He burst into the old kitchens and forced himself to take a straight path to the door. There was quite a bit of old furniture piled up along with other nooks and crannies and crumbled walls where someone could be hiding. Rose might be there, and the urge to find her was almost overwhelming.

But she would be safest if he could get the men behind him out of the house. Stopping to look for her would only put everyone in more danger. And he'd already done enough to condemn them all.

He had no idea what he'd do once he got outside. There were at least six men on his tail. He could never defeat so many on his own. But it didn't matter anymore. As long as he bought enough time for the others to reach safety, that's all that mattered. He neared the door and turned around, waiting to be sure the others were coming after him.

Thomas and his crew crashed into the kitchen, and Will sprinted for the door. He squinted against the sudden brightness of the sun but didn't stop. He needed a plan.

Movement from the corner of his eye caught his attention, and he looked toward the small copse of trees that sat toward the back of the manor. Rose and Lady Alice were on either side of Lady Elizabet, helping support her as they ran for the trees. There was a shout, and Will saw Ramsay rein in his horse and run into the trees with two men.

No!

Will cursed and took two steps in that direction. But Thomas, Murphy, and the rest of their men spilled out of the kitchen doorway and Will stopped, his chest heaving.

Every cell in his body screamed at him to run after Rose, protect her from the devil who threatened her. But if he did so, he'd lead six more men straight to her. As it stood now, there were only three men chasing the women. All the women were armed. They wouldn't be a match for Ramsay and his men, but they could hold them off for a little bit. Hopefully, long enough for John's men to reach them.

If Will followed, he'd only be bringing more of the enemy.

No. He must lead them away from Rose. As far as he could.

He picked up a stone from the crumbling wall and bellowed in fury, throwing it at the men following him. All the rage and anguish building in him fueled his strength, and the stone felled one of the men, dropping him to the ground with a spray of blood.

Will turned and ran.

He dashed for an old rundown silo that sat in the shadow of the manor. The men were close behind him and he ran faster, his legs burning and trembling beneath him. He pushed inside the door and took quick stock of his surroundings. A stone staircase wound its way around the inside wall of the building, though there was a large gap about halfway up. There wasn't much else on the inside aside from piles of stone from the dilapidated walls.

A slight breeze on the back of his neck was the only warning he had that someone was upon him. He spun, his sword already poised to counter the blow. The blades clashed with a clang that rang in his ears. He stumbled back a few feet. The stones under his feet shifted, knocking him off-balance. He blocked another blow, barely. Dust choked him and made his eyes water, but he kept swinging at his opponent. He wasn't even sure who he fought. It didn't matter. There would be another to take his place if Will managed to fell him.

"There's no escape for you, Butler. Or MacGregor, whoever you are. Give up now and maybe we'll kill you quickly. If not, we'll give you to the master and let him punish you as he sees fit."

Will coughed and gripped his sword in both hands, finally getting a good look at who he fought. Thomas.

He shook his head. "We dinna have to fight each other, Thomas. I always liked ye. Ye're a decent man, aside from who ye work for."

"Sorry, mate," Thomas said. "Unlike you, I'm no traitor."

"I guess that settles it then." Will swung again, this time forcing Thomas back a few paces. Enough that Will had some room.

Being on the stairs wasn't ideal, but Murphy was creeping up on him from the side, and he couldn't let himself be flanked by the men or there'd be no escape.

Thomas followed him up the stairs and lunged. They were done talking. Will swung, climbed a step, swung again. He wasn't winning, but neither was Thomas. He was running out of stairs. The gap was only a few steps away. And both men knew it.

"You're out of stairs," Thomas said with a cold grin.

"Aye, I noticed."

He glanced down below. Murphy and another man stalked him, swords ready to attack if Will jumped. He cursed as Thomas tried to force him, blow by blow, toward the gap.

Will had three options. Throw himself at Thomas in the hope he could knock him off-balance and down the stairs without breaking his own neck or getting skewered in the process. Jump from the stairs and take his chances with the two men who stood ready and waiting below.

Or a third option, which was even worse than the first two and had less of a chance for survival. But it would take out more men. He wouldn't think about the fact that one of those men would most assuredly be him. He took a deep breath and gripped his sword tight. If he was going to die, he might as well take as many of his enemy with him as he could.

Thomas raised his arm to strike again, and Will took his chance. He swiped his hand across the crumbling wall of the silo, sending a shower of gravel and dust into Thomas's face. Thomas howled, grabbing for his eyes, and Will kicked out, his foot catching Thomas right in the gut and sending him tumbling backward down the stairs.

The men below shouted and scrambled, one running for Thomas, the other circling below where Will stood on the stairs. Will raised his sword in both hands and threw it as hard as he could at the man standing below. The man raised an arm to protect himself from the blade, but not in time. The sword sank into his shoulder, and he dropped with a scream.

Murphy turned away from where Thomas lay unmoving at the bottom of the stairs and looked at the man screaming on the floor. He went to him, and Will jumped, grabbing at the beam that ran across the width of the building above his head. His hands slipped on the dust-covered wood, but it gave him enough of a swing to use the momentum to slam into Murphy, knocking him to the ground as he broke his fall.

The landing sent sharp jarring pain through his legs and up into his back and he rolled, gasping to catch his breath. Murphy lay crumpled on the floor. But their shouts had drawn the attention of the men outside. Will had only seconds.

He stumbled to his feet, pulled his sword from the shoulder of the man who now lay quiet and gasping on the floor, and ran for the back of the building. His legs hurt with every step, but nothing was broken. He couldn't stop.

Sunlight streamed through some stones at the back, and Will threw his body into them, grunting with the pain that shot through him at the impact. But the stones loosened. Twice more he threw his body into them before they gave, tumbling him outside in a pile of rubble.

The horses were only yards away. He prayed he could make it. He prayed Rose and her ladies still lived. Prayed someone would make it to them before it was too late.

He stumbled and ran toward the horses when a fiery burst of pain dropped him to his knees. A dagger jutted out from his side, and another man ran toward him. He grasped the dagger and pulled it from his body with a yell. The man was almost upon him. He stayed on his knees, head down, watching from the corner of his eye. When the man was almost on top of him, sword raised for a killing blow, Will spun and struck upward, driving the dagger straight into the man's heart.

The man fell. Will dragged himself to his feet, hunched over and clutching his side to protect the knife wound. He staggered toward the horses and had barely managed to drag himself into the saddle when two more men raced toward him.

He turned the horse south and spurred it forward. The more men he could lead away from Kirkenroch, the better. He was done for. His life's blood drained from his side and out of his arm. His body ached from the battering it had taken. He wanted nothing more than to lie down and die. But Kirkenroch, and Rose, were still in danger. In danger because of him.

He'd done this. He'd led these men to the gates. It had been his word that had sent half of Kirkenroch's fighting force to defend the wrong castle. His mistake in taking Rose, a disastrous decision that had not only given Ramsay the clues he needed but had probably led Rose to her death with her mistress when she should have been safe at home, far away in London.

He could never atone for his mistakes. But he could give his life to defend those he'd wronged. He could only pray it would be enough. That he was able to remove enough men that Kirkenroch's men would have a chance to defend their gates until help could arrive.

Horse hooves thundered behind him and he kicked his horse into a faster run, ignoring the jarring motions that sent fresh waves of agony through his body.

He led them into the forest, toward his cottage. The trees and undergrowth grew thick there. There were few trails and many opportunities to lead the men following him into danger. He risked a glance behind him. Six men gave chase, and he smiled, despite the pain wracking him. They were fools. But he was a traitor in their eyes. They'd want to capture him, see him punished.

Good. Their hatred would lead them all to their deaths.

And then he could go to the cottage and await his own.

Chapter Thirteen

He wasn't back yet. And he wasn't coming back. Rose knew it, deep down. Whether he was dead or too wounded or too damn stubborn, he wasn't coming back.

Unless she found him and dragged him back. And he was a fool if he thought she wouldn't.

"Stop fidgeting, lass," the housekeeper said. The woman had been kindly tending to Rose's wounds. Thankfully, they weren't bad. Scrapes and bruises. An eye that was blackening nicely. Nothing that would stop her from going after William.

"I'm sorry," she said, jumping up. "But I must go."

"And where do ye think ye're running off to?"

"I have to go after William. He was wounded. He'll need help."

"Och, leave that to the menfolk, lass. They'll find him right enough."

Rose shook her head. They might find him. They might not. Either way, she couldn't sit there waiting.

"Well, if ye insist, take these with ye," the housekeeper said, shoving her sewing kit at Rose. "And these as well."

She helped her gather as much as she could, everything they thought she'd need. Bandages and needle and thread in case he was wounded. A bit of food. And a bottle of whisky that sent a pang of guilt through her to take. But she stashed that in her bundle as well. William would need it. And if he didn't, she would.

She wished she had her dagger, but she hadn't seen it since she'd given it to Lady Alice.

Within a few minutes she was ready. She took a deep breath and went to speak to her mistress. She pushed away the guilt that flooded her at the thought of Lady Alice. Rose was supposed to stay with her. Guard her. Serve her. Leaving her felt wrong. But William out in the wilds on his own, maybe hurt, maybe dying...

Rose shook her head. She had to go.

She hurried to her mistress's door and raised her arm to knock. But before she could, the door opened, revealing a startled Alice.

"Rose? What is it?" Alice asked, her voice full of concern.

"My pardon, my laird, my lady," Rose said with a small curtsy and nod to each of them, "but I must beg your permission to leave for a short time. I would never ask, but I have no choice."

Alice frowned but answered, "Of course, you may have as long as you need."

"Thank you, my lady," she said, relief flooding through her. She went at once to the small room off the main chamber where she'd been sleeping and began to pack.

"Only please tell me what is wrong," Alice said, following her. "Perhaps I can help."

"Is Rose here?" She could hear Elizabet asking from the main chamber. "The housekeeper said she sat still barely long enough to have her wounds tended and then announced she had to go save William."

Alice looked at her, surprised. "Rose?"

She sighed and glanced up. "William has not yet returned, and there has been no word from him. The search party doesn't know where to look. I do."

"Then tell us, lass," Philip said. "We'll send men—"

"You can't spare them," she said, adding a "sir," with wide eyes when she remembered whom she addressed. "I can find him quicker, with less trouble to the rest of the house."

John strode back to the chamber door and called out to one of the young lads who was always nearby to do his laird's bidding. After a quick exchange the boy ran off, and John came back to the group.

Rose ignored them, shoving a few more provisions in her saddlebags and checking back through them to make sure she had everything she could possibly need. She knew she probably seemed churlish. Or crazy. But the urgency ate at her. If she didn't leave soon, she'd start to panic.

"Are you sure you wish to do this?" Alice asked her as Elizabet tucked extra supplies into the bags. "At least wait for morning."

"I cannot," Rose said. "He's already been missing for several hours, and he was wounded. He would have returned by now if he could."

Alice and Elizabet exchanged a glance, and Rose jutted her chin in the air. "I know what everyone thinks. But you don't know William as I do. The man is as stubborn as they come and not nearly intelligent enough to give up and die like a normal man. He's out there suffering somewhere. I owe the fool. And so, I'm going to find him and bring him home, so he can suffer in peace."

Philip looked at her, with a curious but understanding expression. Then he nodded and went over to her. He handed her a small dagger. Her dagger. The one she'd given Alice. The one William couldn't stop stealing from her. She choked back the sob that threatened to erupt and nodded her thanks at him before slipping it into the pocket of her skirt.

"Young Rob is armed as well," John said, nodding to the stable boy who had joined them and who stood, slightly nervous-looking but determined.

"I'll accompany ye, miss," he said.

Rose wanted to protest but didn't have a good reason to refuse his help. And he might come in handy if William was too wounded to move on his own. Finally, she nodded and murmured her thanks. Elizabet gave her a quick kiss on her cheek and wished her Godspeed before being whisked off to bed by an impatient and disapproving midwife.

Rose gathered her things, and everyone else accompanied her to the courtyard. John pulled young Rob aside for some last-minute instructions, so Rose mounted her horse and nodded at each of them.

"If you're not back by tomorrow, we'll send riders out after you," Alice said. "I understand your wish to find William, but I don't want to lose you as well."

Rose nodded. "I understand. The place I'm thinking of isn't too far from here. If he's not there then…" She shrugged, and her face felt numb, as if all the blood had drained from it. She took a deep breath and straightened her shoulders, forcing a sense of calm she didn't really feel. She gripped the reins. "I'll be back soon. Or will send word," she promised, glancing at Rob.

Then she turned her horse and led it over to where Rob now waited.

• • •

"There it is," Rose said, pointing to the almost obscured clearing up ahead.

"That's just a ruin, miss," Rob said. "Surely no one is in

there."

Rose didn't answer. She wasn't going to argue with him. A group of Ramsay's men had been seen chasing a lone rider in this direction. The search party hadn't seen any sign of Will on the way there, though they had found one horse wandering back toward Kirkenroch. There was no way of knowing if it had been the one Will had taken or not, but Rose thought it likely. If he were wounded and looking for a place to lay low, this is where he'd come. And that is where she'd go as well, no matter anyone else's opinion.

She brought her horse up to the fallen wall they'd used when they'd passed through before, and dismounted. Rob followed her, but he didn't look very happy about it. She hurried to the door and pushed it open, cautiously peeking inside. It took everything in her not to barge in, but there was really no telling who or what might be there, if anything. The last thing she wanted to do was spook some animal or surprise an enemy who may have taken shelter there.

The sound of a gun cocking echoed through the small space, and a sliver of sunlight from the open door glinted off the barrel of a pistol.

"Go away if ye dinna wish to be shot," a gravelly, raw voice said from the shadows.

She'd know that voice anywhere.

"Will," she said, pushing her way in, ignoring Rob's restraining hand on her arm.

Will was lying on the pallet he'd made up for her when they'd ridden through a few days before. Had it been only a few days? It felt like a lifetime ago.

She stood over him, hands on her hips, and waited for him to lower the gun.

He squinted up at her. "Rose?" he croaked.

"Yes. Would you like to put the pistol down now?"

He snorted. "May as well. 'Tis no' loaded anyhow."

She rolled her eyes, but her heart was thumping in fear, racing with excitement, and clenching with dread at his obviously wounded state. She felt like running out the door and vomiting her breakfast into the flowerbed. Not that she'd let him see that.

She took a deep breath and got to work.

She sent Rob out to get her bags and dropped to her knees by Will to assess the damage. Once Rob had brought her what she needed, she sent him out again for wood and set him to making a fire. Will's clothing had stuck to his wounds and she wet the material down with water in an attempt to loosen it, rather than rip it away. She didn't want to start a fresh flood of blood if she could help it.

Will lay there, watching her, his over-bright eyes the only part of his body that reacted as they followed every move she made. He was drenched in sweat but shivered as if he were cold. That, combined with the amount of blood he'd obviously lost, terrified her, though she tried not to let him see how much.

She failed. She didn't even realize she was crying until he reached up and wiped the tears from her cheek with a trembling hand.

"I dinna deserve yer tears, lass."

His voice, quiet and broken, destroyed the last bit of control she had. She dropped to his side, pressing her face into the crook of his neck as she sobbed. He held her close, stroking her back and murmuring Gaelic nonsense into her ear. His lips brushed against her temple, then her cheek, and she turned to him, meeting his lips with all the pent-up emotion she'd tried to keep hidden.

All the fear from the last few days. All the worry. All the pain. All the relief to find him still alive. And the unspoken terror that he might not be for much longer. She gave it all to him. And he took it. His mouth moved over hers like a starving man who'd been offered a lifesaving feast. Every touch of his lips, every swipe of his tongue, filled her with life, strength. Hunger. And another emotion she wasn't ready to confront yet.

She finally tore her lips from his and rested her forehead on his shoulder, dragging in one ragged breath after another while she fought for control. He was hurt. Maybe dying. And even if he wasn't, she couldn't...they couldn't...

She pushed away, ignoring his soft call. "Lass..."

She stood and brushed her hands down her skirt, then across her cheeks, wiping away the last remnants of her tears. Breaking down like that was unforgivable. Giving in... couldn't happen again.

"Rose," he said, but she wouldn't meet his eyes.

"Where are the men who were chasing you?" she asked.

She thought he might have laughed, but the sound came out as more of a croak. "I dinna ken for some of them. One fell off his horse. He must ha' been wounded already. Or a horrible rider."

He broke off and coughed, then groaned, grabbing his side.

She immediately dropped back to her knees beside him, gently moving his hands so she could peel up his shirt. Her breath caught in her throat, but she took care not to make a sound. The wound wasn't large, thank heaven, but it was deep. The angry, red edges of it puckered around the gaping hole that oozed his life away.

"One of the other men stopped, I think, to help the one who fell," Will murmured.

Rose made some noncommittal noise and rummaged in the bundle the housekeeper had given her for a needle and thread. There were also packets of herbs and fresh bandages. She took the herbs out and smelled them. One she was pretty sure was willow bark. That was good for pain and fever. The others…she didn't know.

She didn't realize she was frowning down at the herbs in her hands until Will reached out a trembling hand and pointed to one of the bundles she held.

"Make that one into a poultice," he said. "To put on the wound."

"You know what these are for?" she asked, relief spilling through her.

He nodded. "My granny was a healer," he said, his voice faint. "And ye'd be surprised how much knowledge ye pick up when ye ride with highwaymen and mercenaries. Men who are wounded often need to tend to themselves, ye ken?"

She nodded, choking back tears. She called for Rob, who had thankfully made himself scarce earlier. He poked his head back in the door and hurried over when she directed him to make a tea of the willow bark and a poultice of the others. Then she grabbed the whisky out of the bag.

"Ah, thank Christ," Will said, lifting his head so she could pour some into his mouth.

"Take another," she urged. "This is going to hurt."

"What will?"

His question choked off in a strangled gasp when she poured the whisky over the wound.

"Sorry," she murmured. She had no idea if that was the right thing to do or not, but she knew the wound should be clean before she sewed it up, and the whisky seemed a better choice than the water from the stream that Rob had brought in.

She set to work stitching the wound closed. If someone had told her a month ago she'd be sewing more flesh than stockings she'd have laughed. At this point, she'd give anything for a nice petticoat to hem. Anything other than Will's torn flesh.

"I shot two o' them," Will said through clenched teeth.

"What?" she asked, looking up in surprise.

His face was pale and beads of sweat lined his brow, but he seemed lucid enough.

"The other men who were chasing me," he said between heavy breaths. "I shot two of them."

"Where did you get the pistols? And if you had them, why didn't you give me one? It would have come in handy when Ramsay showed up," she said with a wry smile.

Will grabbed her hand, and she stopped sewing so she could clasp his hand tight. "I'm sorry, lass," he said. "That ye had to face him on yer own. My fault…"

"No." She shook her head. "None of this was your fault." She squeezed his hand and repeated that more firmly at the look of obvious disbelief on his face. "None of this, Will. Do you hear me? The only person responsible for this mess was Ramsay. Who I'm delighted to inform you is dead."

Will raised a brow at that. "Ye bloodthirsty wee thing. Ye killed him, did ye?"

She laughed. "No. Lady Elizabet did. Shot him dead. With a pistol in each hand."

"Heh." A faint smile crossed his lips, and he laid his head back and closed his eyes. "Where did she get the pistols?"

"I'm not sure, actually. One she already had in her pocket. I felt it bump against my leg when we were running. The other she either already had or she took it off one of the men attacking us. Perhaps Ramsay himself. He was certainly arrogant enough to underestimate her."

He smiled again. "Clever lassie."

"That she is," Rose said. "Now hold still."

"I would have given ye the pistols if I'd found them sooner," he murmured. "They were on the horse I took."

"You have two?"

His head twitched slightly in a shake. "Dropped one after I used it. Kept the other. Thought maybe I could find more ammunition once I stopped."

"Ah," she said, putting in the final stitch. "And did you find more?" She bit off the stitch and sat back to grab the whisky and some bandages.

"No. The other two bastards either got lost or gave up the chase. Either way, they werena with me when I arrived. And I didna feel like exploring just then."

"I bet," she said, pouring more of the whisky over the now-closed wound.

Will cried out again and panted a few times, his breath hissing out between his teeth. "Christ, woman. Stop doing that!"

"Stop running into daggers and I'll consider it." She handed him the bottle and let him drink a few more mouthfuls while she bandaged up his side with the poultice Rob handed her.

"Now let me see what you've done to your arm."

That one wasn't as bad. Some of the stitches had come undone, but the bleeding wasn't too concerning so she redressed it before checking over the rest of him.

Rob handed her a cup of the willow bark tea, and she helped Will sit up enough to drink it. He grimaced at the taste but she made him drink as much as he could hold. She didn't like how pale his skin was, how weak his hand when he tried to squeeze hers, or the heat that radiated off him.

It didn't take him long to fall asleep. She expected him to be restless, either because of the pain or the fever. But he slept heavily. Too heavily. The sight of it sent an icy fear creeping through her. But despite it all, his chest continued to rise and fall. Not as strongly as she'd like. But as long as breath remained in his body, she wouldn't complain too loudly.

"How is he, miss?" Rob asked as he handed her a cup of tea he'd brewed.

"I don't know. Not good. We need to get him back to

Kirkenroch. But..." She glanced out the open door.

It was growing late. She didn't want to move him in the dark. She didn't know the land well enough. They'd need some way to transport him, in any case. He wouldn't be able to sit a horse by himself, and she didn't have the strength to get him on one in any case. Even with Rob's help. He was a good and helpful lad, but he wasn't much bigger than she.

"I should ride for help, miss. Bring men back to carry him home. We can fashion a litter. My laird will ken what to do."

She nodded, but her glance strayed to the darkening skies beyond the door. She didn't want to send Rob off into the night alone. Kirkenroch wasn't too far, but it was a good couple hours' ride.

The need to get Will help before he got worse beat at her in a frantic panic. But it wouldn't do any of them any good if Rob got lost in the night or somehow injured himself and his horse.

Finally, she sighed. "We'll stay here tonight. It's too late to do anything now." Before he could argue she held up a hand. "In the morning, you can ride back to Kirkenroch and bring help."

Rob didn't look convinced but nodded, nonetheless. "I'll go get more firewood."

"Thank you, Rob."

She sat beside Will until her eyes grew heavy. Rob took care of the horses and then puttered around the cottage, making sure there was water simmering over the fire and more wood when they needed it. And he helped her change Will's poultice and bandage twice. Will didn't wake again.

But he still breathed. She took comfort in that, small comfort...but for how long, she couldn't say.

Rob wrapped himself in his kilt and curled up on the other side of the cottage by the fire. Weariness pulled at Rose, and she knew she should get some rest as well. She wouldn't be any good to Will if she was too tired to help him. But she was afraid to sleep. Afraid that if she wasn't awake to watch the rise and fall of his chest, that it would stop.

Finally, she curled up by Will's uninjured side, her back to the fire, and lay as close to him as she could. She made sure the drape of his kilt covered them both, and then layered her cloak over the top of that so she could share her warmth with him. Then she laid her hand lightly on his chest and watched her fingers rise and fall, rise and fall, until she couldn't keep her eyes open any longer.

Chapter Fourteen

At first light, Rose saw Rob off.

"Are you sure you remember the way?" she asked him for probably the third time.

"Aye, miss. This thicket is well hidden if ye dinna ken what ye're looking for, but once I'm out of this tangle, it's a straight journey north to Kirkenroch."

She nodded, absently patting the horse's neck. Sending the lad off on his own sat ill with her. He wasn't really much younger than her. Still, if there'd been any other choice... But there wasn't. Will needed help.

"All right, then. Off you go." She forced a smile and stood back.

He nodded and turned the horse, but she ran forward again and he stopped, eyebrows raised in question.

"Be careful," she said. "Ramsay was defeated but it's possible some of his men are still about."

He smiled down at her. "Aye, miss. I'll be most careful."

She smiled and stood back, lifting her hand in farewell as the horse slowly pushed through the bushes and trees that hid the small cottage from sight.

She watched the spot where they'd disappeared until she could no longer hear them and then took a deep breath, lifting her head to the weak morning sunlight. Will's bandage would need changing soon, and she didn't want to leave him long. But she also needed to gather more willow bark. Rob had shown her where to get more, along with a few more herbs that might aid in healing Will's wounds. She'd get those before she went back in. And with any luck, Rob would be back with help before nightfall.

She untied her horse and turned to lead him down to the stream. He could drink and graze while she foraged, and he would make carrying everything back much easier.

A gunshot rang out, echoing through the forest. Her horse reared, yanking the leads from her hands and taking off at a dead run, crashing through the thick foliage around their clearing. She cursed under her breath. Damn that horse! And whoever had scared him off.

Her blood ran cold. Who had it been? She crouched down, her heart pounding frantically. While the loss of the horse was devastating, she prayed it would run off instead of returning. If it returned home, at least it would alert everyone that they needed help, even if it couldn't lead them back to the cottage. But if it returned to the cottage, it might lead whoever had shot that gun right to them.

"Rob," she whispered.

She glanced back at the cottage door, but there was no sound from within. She waited a few more seconds. No one came through the trees. No other sounds floated to her on the wind. The woods were silent once again.

Still she waited, arguing with herself what she should do. The thought of leaving Will, even for a few minutes, tore her to shreds. But Rob...if he'd run into any of Ramsay's men, he could be hurt. Dying. Or already dead. She couldn't leave him to suffer alone if that was the case. And she had to know. If Rob had been wounded or killed, there would be no help coming from Kirkenroch. She'd need to make plans…

Finally, she took a deep breath. Sitting there cowering wasn't going to help anyone.

"Move," she muttered to herself, forcing her terror-frozen limbs to get up. She hurried into the cottage and quickly checked on Will.

He hadn't moved at all but still lay in the fever-induced stupor he'd fallen into the night before. She tucked his kilt about him and made sure he was fully covered. Then she kicked some dirt over the fire. There was only a tiny thread of smoke rising from it through the small hole in the ceiling, but she didn't want to take the chance that someone might see it and be led to the cottage.

She wrapped her cloak tightly about her and went into the woods, following the path Rob had taken. Taking care to make no sound, she moved slowly, staying hidden in the trees and bushes. Every few steps she'd stop and listen. But the only sound she heard was her own breathing.

Finally, she came to a spot where the trees were thinner, creating a small clearing. There was evidence that several horses had been through. But there were none about now. No men either, but there were boot prints in the mud.

And no Rob.

She remained hunched in the bushes, debating if she should explore further or give up and go back to Will. The shot could have come from anyone. Perhaps Rob was shooting to scare off an animal. Yet another reason she should get back to the cottage. And if he'd been shooting at an enemy, she didn't want to stick around and see who it was. The thought of Rob needing help was the only thing that made her decide to stay for a few more minutes. She couldn't risk going farther out into the clearing. From that point on, the trees thinned out and there wouldn't be any place for her to hide.

She'd finally determined to go back to the cottage when a raspy sigh stopped her. Heart thudding in her ears, she listened again. It was coming from several yards away. She crept closer, her dagger tight in her hand. A boot stuck out from under one of the bushes, and she eased over. Whoever it was didn't seem to be in a position to threaten her.

With a final glance around to make sure there was no one else nearby, she finally pushed through the remaining bushes and uncovered the man lying on the forest floor.

"Rob," she gasped, dropping to her knees beside him.

He blinked up at her when he heard his name. "Miss Rose?"

Her hands quickly searched him, looking for his wound.

Wounds, it turned out. A shallow dagger wound on his forearm where he'd blocked a blow aimed for his neck. And a more concerning wound from the pistol shot in his thigh.

She closed her eyes and cursed under her breath. What more could possibly happen to them?

"Who did this?" she asked.

He snorted. "I'm no' sure. Ramsay's men, mayhap. There were three of them. Came at me from nowhere. They wanted the horse. One o' them slashed at me, cut my arm and managed to knock me from the saddle. When I tried to run after them, one of them shot me. Then the other horse charged through. Was it yers?"

Rose nodded and he sighed. "I thought it might be. They were worried about where it had come from, but they werena in any shape to be fighting for it if the owner came looking. They grabbed both horses and left. Or seemed to. I couldna be sure. I didna want to lead them back to ye. They didna seem keen to stay in the area, but I thought to hide here until I was sure they were gone. Just in case. But I must have… must have fallen asleep…maybe…"

"Shh," Rose said, pulling the scarf from her neck to wrap around his leg. It wasn't the cleanest cloth. But it would have to do until she got him back to the cottage.

"Can you walk if I help you?" she asked.

Rob stared at her, his pale face pinched with determination. "Aye, miss."

She nodded and pocketed her dagger, then looped an arm around his back. It took them a few moments, but they got him on his feet. Getting him back to the cottage was another matter. The forest growth was thick, and there were several places where Rose had to let Rob go and resort to pulling and dragging to help him get through. They were slowed even more by Rob's insistence they obscure their trail as they moved. She understood the reason and even heartily agreed. But it took time. And every second away from Will stoked her anxiety until she was nearly at her breaking point by the time they reached the cottage.

She managed to get Rob inside and settled on his pallet from the night before. Then she hurried to Will's side. He still breathed. He was far too pale aside from his fever-flushed cheeks. But he lived. Considering their circumstances, that was almost more than she dared to hope.

She sat back on her heels, pressing her hand to her forehead while she took a couple of deep breaths. The pit of panic in her chest squeezed like a vise, and she focused on staying calm. They couldn't afford for her to lose it now. Both men needed care. And help wasn't coming.

"Right, then," she muttered, getting to her feet.

First things first. She needed to get Rob patched up and comfortable. Then she should probably get more tea into Will. And she needed to gather more herbs, especially as Rob would be needing them as well. And food. They needed food.

The panic threatened to spill over again, and she swallowed hard against the tears that burned in her throat.

She desperately longed for her old life when the most she had to worry about was whether Lady Alice would like the new hairstyle Rose had fashioned for her, or occasionally helping Cook in the kitchen. But she wasn't home. She was in the middle of nowhere with two wounded men who were depending on her for their lives. So she tried to push any other thoughts from her mind. There was no time for that.

She took off her petticoat and ripped a strip from it. She'd shred the rest once she'd gotten Rob taken care of. Between him and Will, she'd need every inch of cloth she had.

She cleansed his wounds, thanking whatever saints were listening that they weren't worse. The cut on his arm wasn't deep enough to need stitching, thankfully. So she cleaned it the best she could and wrapped it tightly.

His leg wound was another matter. The ball had gone straight through, so at least she didn't have to dig for it. But it had done a messy job when it had passed through. Again, she cleaned and bandaged it as best she could.

"Thank ye, miss," Rob said, his voice quiet and strained. "I'm sorry I couldna help…"

"Oh, hush," she said, handing him a cup of cold willow bark tea left over from that morning. "It wasn't your fault those men were still in the woods. Hopefully, they are gone now."

"Aye, I think they are," he said, grimacing as he sipped. "With their master gone, they have no reason to stick about. Several of their men were wounded as well. I think that is the only reason they were still here. With our horses, they'll travel that much faster."

He grimaced again, and Rose patted his hand.

"Get some rest. I'm going to gather some more of those herbs that you showed me. I won't be long."

He nodded. "I'll keep watch over Will until ye return."

She knew she should insist he sleep, but knowing he'd be

there to keep an eye on Will lifted a huge weight from her shoulders. So instead of protesting, she nodded and patted his hand.

She didn't tarry outside but gathered as many herbs and plants as she could in a few minutes and immediately returned.

She didn't want to light a fire, too afraid the smoke might draw anyone who still lingered in the forest. But she needed hot water to make tea for both men and to cleanse their wounds. Finally, deciding the benefits were worth the risk, she lit a small fire. But she didn't sleep a wink that night, jumping at every sound. By morning, when the only things to invade their clearing were a few birds and a rabbit or two, she relaxed enough to doze fitfully by Will's side. She didn't touch him again, though, except for when she needed to tend to him. The rush of emotion that had overwhelmed her upon her first sight of him remained. Strengthened, even, with every passing day. But giving in would do little good for either of them.

If Will survived, he'd be returning to John's side. Or maybe the clan would send him out on some other fool's errand. Either way, it would take him in the opposite direction of where Rose belonged. With Lady Alice, who would surely wish to return home after all the danger and heartache of the last few weeks. If she decided to stay with Philip in Scotland… Rose wasn't sure what she would do.

Her place was with Lady Alice. But she'd never truly considered leaving London permanently. Scotland had its beauty. But it was a wild, untamed place compared to the city of her birth. And now more than ever, Rose longed for the familiarity of her home.

The next week was a haze of caring for both men. Rob was lucid enough to talk her through setting a trap for small game, and on the second night she managed to catch a fat rabbit. Skinning and dressing it for cooking wasn't her favorite task and certainly wasn't something she'd ever had to do before. But once her belly was full of the delicious roasted meat, her squeamishness over the task dissipated greatly.

Better still was the broth she made from the animal's bones and some of the herbs she'd found. She managed to get a good portion of it into William. He needed the nourishment desperately, and if it meant skinning a hundred rabbits to keep his cheeks from growing sunken and hollow, she'd do it.

By the second week, Will had improved enough he could sit up, and he stayed awake for longer and longer periods of time. Rob managed to hobble around with the aid of a tree branch he'd found. He still couldn't do much, but he took over herb gathering and animal trapping for Rose. She didn't want him to do too much, but she was grateful for the help. Mostly because it meant she could spend more time with Will.

He'd graduated from eating a mash she'd make of a handful of oats, broth, and whatever meat Rob had found to eating the meat straight from the bone. But he still couldn't stand for more than a few minutes before he broke out in a sweat. Still, the improvement was heartening to her. Anything was better than him lying beside the fire looking pale as death.

And at night when she lay beside him, he now wrapped his arm about her and held her close to his side. They never spoke of it. It never went any further. But each continued to seek out comfort from the other in the dark of night.

As horrible as the last weeks had been, Rose would miss those quiet moments in the night. They couldn't continue once they made it home. She and Will had an unspoken truce while they focused on surviving, but that would surely end once they were safe. She could hardly imagine what life would look like then. They'd done little else since that morning he'd taken her. They'd gone from one danger-laden situation to the next. How would they even interact with each other without death hanging over their heads? The few moments they'd had that were not fraught with danger had been filled with their bickering. Perhaps they could get along only at the point of a gun.

It was a sobering notion. But not one she had to dwell on yet. Will was improving, but he couldn't travel yet. So for now, she'd lay her head on his chest and pretend it was the most natural thing in the world. Thoughts of the future could wait.

Chapter Fifteen

Will's strength returned little by little. Each day he could feel the difference. His side ached a little less. His limbs ceased their trembling every time he moved. His arm was almost back to new. It was the other wound that still gave him trouble. It was healing as well as he could have hoped. There was no sign of infection and, aside from the initial fever the first few days, he'd been mostly lucid. Except he slept more than a newborn babe and felt about as weak.

A circumstance made all the more frustrating because of the beautiful woman who slept by his side every night.

She touched him as little as possible during the day. Something he both hated and appreciated. The heat burning between them grew more unbearable, and there was little he could, or should, do about it. Even if his physical condition was much improved. They both knew that nothing could come of furthering their connection but heartache. He belonged at Kirkenroch, with John. And she…she belonged back in England. Back in the grand houses where she'd grown up, where she'd be safe from marauding villains and surly

Highlanders. Where she could go back to caring for dresses and jewelry instead of bleeding wounds and dying men.

During the day, he reminded himself of all that. Reminded himself that they didn't belong together. That she had a home far from there where she longed to be. That they had responsibilities that pulled them in different directions. Not to mention the sore point she'd never forgive him for. He'd stolen her. Put her in danger. Dragged her from one end of England to the far end of Scotland and had made her life miserable every step of the way.

Even if that weren't the case, he'd proven pretty conclusively that everything he touched, he destroyed. The decisions he made on instinct, like taking her, had turned out disastrously. The decisions he agonized over, thinking over every aspect, like sending Kirkenroch's men to Glenlyon— those turned out even worse. Even if he thought for a split second he and Rose might have something between them, his decisions were the last anyone should follow. He had no right to think of anything but returning Rose to her home.

He had no right to long for anything else. To count the hours until night fell. Because at night...at night, after she'd toiled the day away, she slipped down next to him and rested her head on his shoulder, her hand covering his heart. Perhaps she felt he was too wounded, and she was too tired for there to be any danger of anything more than sleep. Or perhaps after an entire day of staying away, it was too much to do so once the sun set. He didn't care. He knew only that he lived for the moment when she secured the door with the tree branch she'd hauled inside, banked the fire for the night, and wordlessly lay down beside him.

Rose continued to amaze him. Somehow, she'd managed to not only save his life, but Rob's as well. The dainty lady's maid who he'd thought was too soft to do more than fold her mistress's silk stockings was now trapping and skinning game, gutting fish, and sewing up gaping wounds like she'd been born to it. If it hadn't been for her, he'd be dead.

If he were honest, he still wasn't sure how he felt about her saving his life. He'd meant to die. A just punishment in his mind for the harm he'd brought to those he loved. He'd brought the devil to their very door. A solitary death in the woods was nothing more than justice.

But his harpy-tongued guardian angel had swooped in and saved his life, and he'd been too far gone to stop her. And then, for good measure, she'd saved Rob's as well. Despite knowing next to nothing about surviving in the rough, she'd kept them breathing. More than that. She'd made them alive and whole again.

Rob watched her with a sort of worshipful expression that made Will want to throttle the boy within an inch of his life. An overreaction, to be sure. But one he couldn't help. Though he understood the emotion. She was their savior.

By the third week, Rob was able to walk without the aid of his crutch. Mostly. He still used it from time to time, but he didn't totally rely upon it to get around. After a few days of ambling around the cottage without tiring, he seemed to have come to a decision.

"I think I should leave in the morning," he said. "Ye're much better, Will. But ye still willna be able to travel on foot for a week at least yet. Maybe more. But if I make it to Kirkenroch, I can bring back horses."

"But your leg," Rose protested. Will watched her, trying to ascertain if she protested out of a sense of concern for his leg. Or something else. But her expression betrayed nothing but worry that he'd reinjure himself.

"It's much better," Rob pointed out. "Not totally healed yet, no. But I can walk well enough. It might take me a day to reach the manor. Maybe even two. But even with that I'd be able to return with help to get ye home much sooner than if ye waited until ye were fully healed."

Will nodded. It was a good plan, but part of him would be sad to leave the little cocoon they'd made for themselves. He would not be sorry to see Rob go, however. The lad had been a tremendous help. But with Rob gone, there would be only he and Rose, alone in the cottage. It would be nice to finally have some privacy for when they were awkwardly avoiding each other.

Rose still frowned and looked at Will. "Are we sure it's safe?"

He nodded. "Aye. Once Ramsay was felled, there would be no reason for his men to stay and risk their necks. The men of Kirkenroch and Glenlyon would have been sent to search the woods and rout any who remained."

"If that is true, why did they not find us?"

Will waved that off. "As I've told ye before, I've been coming to this place since I was a wee lad. If ye dinna ken what ye're looking for, ye'd pass right by without the faintest idea what was here."

"Yes, but..." Rose frowned and shook her head. "Never mind. If you feel like you can make such a journey..." Her gaze flicked to Will and then back. "We would be very grateful."

"I'm much stronger, miss," Rob assured her. "Ye healed me well."

Rose's cheeks blushed a faint pink, and Will frowned. Then berated himself for it. He couldn't fault the lad for mooning over Rose. She was quite the woman.

The next morning, they helped Rob prepare for his journey. Rose frowned as she handed him the bag she'd packed full of food.

"Will it be enough do you think?" she asked.

"Aye," Will said. "It's about twenty miles to Kirkenroch. Were he fully healed, he could make that distance by nightfall.

As it is, he should still make it by tomorrow. The day after at the latest." He frowned a little, watching while Rob filled his waterskin at the stream that ran by the cottage. "As long as he doesna push himself too hard and takes care to rest that leg, he should reach the manor without too much trouble. Ye've packed him enough food to last a week at least."

Rose snorted softly. "His strength hasn't fully returned yet. It took me weeks to get him back on his feet. I don't want him starving to death so close to home."

Will rested his hand on the back of her neck, and she stiffened at first, but relaxed as he softly massaged her muscles. Rob turned back to them, waterskins full. Will kept his arm about Rose's shoulders until she stepped forward to hand Rob his stick.

"I know you don't think you need it, but you might be grateful for it later in the day."

Rob looked like he wanted to argue but took it from her anyway.

"Be sure to take lots of rests. Don't push yourself," she said. "We've lasted here this long, we'll be fine a few more days. Stay in the trees if you can. I know Ramsay's men should be gone but…"

"I'll be fine, miss," Rob said with a laugh. "I ken well enough how to keep hidden. And I promise I'll not push myself too hard. I'll be back with men and horses before ye've noticed I'm gone."

She nodded, then stood on tiptoe to press a kiss to his cheek. The lad flushed with pleasure, and Will had to resist the urge to yank Rose back to his side. She wasn't his and he certainly had no right to act the part of a jealous husband. But it didn't stop the feeling from gnawing at him.

Rob nodded to him, and a twinge of guilt immediately pierced through the jealous haze. The lad was risking much to bring back help because Will was too weak to help himself.

It might not sit well with him, but that was no excuse to take it out on Rob. Will limped forward and embraced him.

"God go with ye, lad."

Rob nodded, his eyes bright. And then he gave them a little bow and limped out of the clearing.

Rose clasped her hands together and held them against her mouth, watching until he'd disappeared into the brushes.

"And now we wait," she murmured.

"Dinna fear for him, lass. He's strong. Smart. He'll be fine."

"That's what I thought the last time, and he was nearly killed moments later."

Will chuckled. It was far easier to laugh at such a situation once the danger had passed. "There's no sense in worrying o'er something we canna control. If the lad fails, we'll know soon enough. Have a little faith."

She glanced up at him. "How do you think I've managed so far? Faith is all I have."

Will's heart jumped. He brushed her hair from her face, his fingers lingering on her skin. "Not all, lass."

Her eyes grew wider at that, but she didn't pull away. If anything, she drew closer. Her gaze shifted to his lips and her own parted slightly. If ever there was a lass made for kissing, it was this one. With all that fiery spirit in her, all that passion, he could drink her in and be sustained for the rest of his life.

If he were smart, he'd run now. Haul his crippled body after Rob as fast as he could go and leave her far behind him. A headstrong English lass had no place in his world. No place with him, at least. He didn't even know where his place was. At Kirkenroch? Glenlyon? He wasn't needed in such places. Not really. The only time he'd felt useful was when he was with Ramsay's men. And even there, he hadn't been important. Not to them at least. But to his clan, aye, he'd been important. A spy risking his life to gain much-needed information, information that would turn the tides of the war they fought.

And he'd failed. Miserably. He hadn't discovered the information they'd so desperately needed. He'd ignited the spark that started the battle and led the enemy straight to his kin. It had been the lovely woman in his arms who had discovered the location of Ramsay's men. She who had saved him when the enemy first attacked. She who had gotten the ladies of the manor to safety. She who had saved his life.

He wasn't worthy of her. He had no right to kiss her. To touch her at all. Yet still, he cupped her face, drawing his thumb across her lips.

He couldn't resist. His heart screamed out for her and once, just once, he wanted to bask in her light.

"Do ye ken what I dreamed of when the fever had me?" he asked, his voice grown husky even to his own ears.

She shook her head, a fine tremor running through her as he continued to caress her.

"You."

She sucked in a breath, and he leaned down ever so slightly. "I dreamed of you. These eyes staring into mine. These hands touching me," he said, interlacing his fingers with hers. "It was yer voice I heard, pulling me back from death. Telling me to get well. Nay," he said with a deep chuckle, "commanding me to get well."

She smiled at that. "And you obeyed. I didn't think you would."

"I didna think I would, either."

"You're too stubborn."

"Aye, but no more so than you."

"Are we arguing over who is the most stubborn now?" she asked with a little laugh that sent sunshine blazing into his soul.

"No. We'd be arguing until the sun went down."

She looked down at their intertwined fingers and brought them up to her face, rubbing her chin lightly across them. "Why did you listen?"

He frowned slightly, not sure what she was asking.

"Why did you come back to me? There were so many times…" Her breath hitched. His heart broke a little at the sound. "So many times, I didn't think you would. I lay beside you at night so I could feel you breathing, even if I couldn't see it in the dark. Sometimes you would falter, and I didn't know whether you'd take another breath or not. I don't think you wanted to. But you always did. Why?"

His hands slid down to encircle her body and hold her close. "Part of me didna wish to return. It seemed…easier to float away. I was tired of the pain. Tired of the guilt. So…tired."

She frowned, her eyes searching his with tears in their depths.

"But I think, even in my darkest moments, I could hear ye. Feel ye by my side. And I didna wish to leave ye. I ken I dinna deserve ye. But I wanted ye still."

Her mouth parted, and a tear tumbled down her cheek. "Will," she breathed. Then she stood on her toes and pressed her lips to his. So softly he could barely feel more than her breath against his skin. Then again, she kissed him. Firmer. More insistent. And he couldn't hold back anymore.

He pulled her to him and angled his mouth over hers, claiming her lips until she opened to him, her tongue tangling with his in an erotic dance that had him swaying on his feet. They broke apart with a laugh, and he pressed his forehead to hers.

"Perhaps we should go inside," she said.

"Aye. I'm perhaps not quite so steady on my feet as I'd hoped."

"Then we should get you to bed."

He blinked at her, surprised. He'd thought perhaps she'd

turn shy as so many women were wont to do. But not his Rose. She took his hand in hers and led him inside, straight to his pallet.

Then she sank down to her knees and lifted a hand for him to join her. He did, lowering himself carefully so as not to jostle his side overmuch. The minute he was seated, Rose climbed on his lap, her legs straddling his. She watched him carefully as if trying to gauge his reaction to her boldness. In answer, he wrapped one arm about her waist to draw her close and cupped the back of her neck so he could drag her lips back to his.

He'd never been with a woman who was so forward, and her confidence as she touched him sent a flaming fire through his blood. Had there ever been a more perfect woman?

Her hands tangled in his hair as they kissed and his hands explored the planes of her back, down to her waist and back up to grasp her shoulders. He twisted, thinking to roll her beneath him but broke off with a gasp and a curse as burning pain shot through his side.

"Are you all right?" she asked, through kiss-swollen lips.

"Aye." He took a couple shallow breaths, waiting for the worst of the pain to subside. "I forgot I was wounded."

She laughed, the husky, passion-tinged sound reverberating through him. She pressed against him, her arms going back around his neck. "I suppose we'll have to make do like this." She rocked against him and leaned forward to capture his lips again.

He groaned, his body burning as if his fever had returned. He needed her. Craved her. She was a dream made real, and if it was not but the fever playing tricks with his mind he wanted nothing more than to be consumed and to never wake again.

Still, when her fingers went to her bodice and began to pull at her laces, he covered her hands with his.

"Are ye sure, lass?"

Chapter Sixteen

Her eyes searched his and she smiled and leaned forward to press a devastating kiss to his lips. "Yes, I'm sure."

"Ye deserve a better place than this." He looked around the cottage, and her heart clenched that he cared so much.

She cupped his face, bringing his gaze back to her. "The place doesn't matter. Only the person I'm with."

"And ye are aware who ye're with?" he asked with a wry grin.

Her laughter pealed out, and she kissed him again. "Yes," she said, rocking against the hard length that was pressed between them. "I'm sure." His hands tightened on her waist, and he groaned against her mouth.

"Are you?" she asked.

His deep chuckle sent waves of pleasure through her body, and this time he pulled her against him. "I've never been more sure of anything in my life. I have been waiting my whole life for a woman as perfect as you. There is no one else I'll ever want."

He kissed her until she whimpered under the onslaught

of his lips.

"I'm not perfect." She kissed his neck. "Not even close." She nibbled at his ear and he pulled at the neckline of her bodice to kiss a path along her collarbone.

"We'll have to agree to disagree." His teeth lightly scraped the delicate skin behind her ear and she grabbed at his shirt, carefully pulling it over his head and then tossing it to the side.

"We can't stand each other, remember," she said, running her hands down his chest, though she took care to stay away from his wounded side.

"Aye. Ye're stubborn. And opinionated. And ye talk too much."

She gasped, not sure if it was in outrage or pleasure. He dragged her against his thigh again and a moan escaped her lips. Pleasure. Definitely pleasure. She'd be outraged later.

"But ye're still perfect. And I'm the luckiest man in the world," he said as his hands slid up her thighs and pulled her as close to him as she could get before returning to her bodice. "You, however," he kissed her again, his fingers making quick work of her bodice laces, "could do much better."

That startled a laugh out of her that was immediately choked off when his lips closed around her breast.

"Oh," she said, though the sound was more of a choked breath than a word. "I think you underestimate yourself."

He chuckled again and took her hand, pressing it to the hard length beneath his kilt. "Och, there's nothing underestimated about me, lass."

Her hands closed around him, and his head dropped back, his breath hissing from his lips. She released him long enough to remove his belt and unwind his kilt, leaving him bare to her gaze. She'd seen him before, of course, as she'd tended to him when he lay dying. But this was different. So very different.

She stood and pulled off the rest of her bodice and skirt. He looked up at her like he was seeing the sun for the first time. Then he reached for her.

"Lie beside me, lass."

She sank down next to him as he carefully rolled to his side. She hitched her leg over his hip, taking care not to brush against his wound. And when he finally entered her, he gasped at the twinge of pain as much as she did.

"Did I hurt ye, lass?" he asked.

"Not much. Did I hurt you?"

"Not much." He chuckled and she gasped again, though not from pain. "We'll have to take this slow, aye?"

She nodded, wanting to touch him everywhere but afraid to at the same time. He grasped her hip, guiding her as they slowly rocked together. The discomfort melted away as they moved, building into something more wonderful than she'd ever dreamed existed.

She grabbed his hip, her fingers digging into his flesh, and he answered her unspoken demand. Some small part of her remembered his wound, worried for it. But the intensity building in her wiped all other thoughts from her mind. There was nothing but him. Moving with her. Through her. Branding himself on her forever.

She'd never be the same again. Even if she walked out of that room and never saw him again, he'd be a part of her soul until the day she died. She'd always been so sure of herself and what she wanted. And with a final stroke, he shattered everything she thought she knew. Her world was gone and a new one, more incredible than anything she'd ever dreamed, was in its place.

He was only a moment behind her and then they held each other, shuddering and gasping for breath.

She finally regained enough presence of mind to remember his side. "Are you hurt? You aren't bleeding again, are you?"

Will laughed and pulled her close for a kiss. "My sweet Rose. I dinna care if I bleed to death right here in this bed. I'd die a happy man."

"Well, I'd care very much." She tried to untangle herself from him, but he held her tight.

"Let it bide, lass. I'm fine. I'll be sore later, for certain. But it was well worth it."

She settled back into his arms, content to believe him. She'd be sure to check his bandages later. But now, she wanted nothing more than to wrap herself around him.

They spent the rest of the day laughing, talking, eating, and exploring all the ways they could enjoy each other. They were both too sore to fully make love again. But Will showed her there was more than one way to find pleasure in each other.

When night fell, they cuddled up together, both lost in their thoughts.

Rob would return, if not the next day then probably the day after. And they would have to return to the world outside their little cottage. A few weeks ago, even a few days ago, there had been nothing that Rose wanted more. Now, she wished they could go on together, just the two of them.

"What are ye thinking about so hard over there?" he asked, pulling her back against his chest.

She sighed happily. "About how much things have changed. And how much they'll change once we go back."

"Why must things change?" he asked, his forehead creasing in a frown.

"Well, they must, mustn't they? Here we've been kind of sheltered from the world. Once we return, we both have responsibilities and obligations…"

He shifted to his back and gazed up at the roof. "I havena given much thought to what will happen when we return. I didna think I'd return at all. Until ye found me and nagged me into living."

She lightly slapped the uninjured part of his chest and he chuckled, taking her hand and bringing it up to his mouth for a kiss.

"Will you stay on at Kirkenroch?" she asked.

"I dinna ken. I lived at Glenlyon before going to England. Then I was with my laird John. Did ye ken he was the Highland Highwayman?"

"I did. But only because Lady Alice likes a bit of gossip, and there was no one else she could trust that bit of information to."

"She shouldna have told anyone. Of course, she must have discovered it from Lady Elizabet. Do lassies do nothing but gossip about that which they shouldna?"

"Oh, and you're one to talk. I've heard the things men say around their campfires. Women aren't nearly so bad."

He snorted. "We'll have to agree to a differing of opinions on that, lass."

"What did you do after being a highwayman?" she asked, steering the conversation back to the relevant matter at hand.

"When John was exiled and his lady ran away with him, I stayed behind and befriended a man in Ramsay's employ. He introduced me to Ramsay and I've been with him ever since. Watching and waiting. Being the eyes and ears for my laird."

"And now that Ramsay's gone?"

He sighed deeply. "I dinna ken. I could go back to Glenlyon. There's always work to be done at the castle. Or most likely I'll stay at Kirkenroch and help them rebuild. John will be in need of good men, and I have been his man since I could swing a sword."

"You'll stay in Scotland then." Rose rested her cheek against his chest, fighting against the sadness settling in her heart. Will hadn't said anything that surprised her. And yet, she had hoped perhaps he might want to return to England. A foolish hope.

"Aye. Will ye no' be staying then?" he asked. "I thought ye'd want to stay with the Lady Alice."

"Of course, I do. But I assumed she'd want to return home. At least at some point. I know that she and Philip... well, I'm not sure what is between them, to be truthful. There was no time to discuss anything after we arrived. But her family is in England. They must be worried for her. And you have to admit, her experiences in Scotland have not been... ideal."

He frowned. "Perhaps not, but that doesna mean she'll wish to abandon her husband and return to her family."

"You are assuming she considers him her husband."

"Why would she not?"

"The way they were married is not a custom that is recognized in England. Her family certainly won't consider her wed, though they may pretend for decency's sake. I'm certain they'll want her to return to them. And if she wishes to go, I must go with her."

"And if she doesna wish to go? If she wishes to stay in Scotland?"

Rose frowned. "I don't know. I've never considered staying. Of course, my place is with Lady Alice. But...I have family in England as well. I...I don't know. I've always been certain Lady Alice would return home. And even if she stays, she'll go where Philip goes. What if he doesn't wish to remain at Kirkenroch? Or even Glenlyon? He might have his own place somewhere else."

Will didn't say anything to that, merely tightened his arms about her and held her close. And Rose didn't say anything else, either. She didn't want to disturb their happy bubble. Because no matter what Will said, Rose didn't see a future in Scotland. She belonged with her lady. And they both belonged back home in England.

Even if her heart yearned to belong to Will.

• • •

They lay in each other's arms, watching the sun rise through the small hole in the cottage's roof. Will brushed Rose's hair off her forehead and pressed a kiss to her brow.

She snuggled in to his chest. "Part of me hoped morning wouldn't come."

He took a deep breath. "It doesna have to be only one night, ye ken."

She sighed. "Will," she said, pressing a kiss to his chest before sitting up. "Nothing has changed since last night. I'm still going back to England with my mistress."

"If she's going. We dinna ken what's transpired between her and my cousin. They are married."

"But not really."

"Aye, they are. And they may wish to remain so."

Rose's slight frown was full of skepticism. "I find that difficult to believe."

"Why?" He tried to ignore the burst of anger that statement created. "Is it so hard to believe an English lass would want to marry a savage Scot, as ye seem fond of calling us?"

Rose chewed at her lip and then sighed again. "Once I would have said yes. But now..." She laughed, but there was little amusement in the sound. "I don't know, Will."

He sat up and cupped her face, drawing her to him for a soft kiss. "Ye dinna believe our two sides can live together in peace?"

"In peace? No."

He laughed and kissed her forehead, pulling her onto his lap so he could wrap his arms about her. "Ye ken well enough what I meant."

"Yes, I know what you meant," she said, playing absently with the hairs on his chest. "But it's not just the two of us. You and I, if we were alone in the world. Yes. I think we could make it work. I hope we could."

His arms tightened about her, though he sensed she wasn't done with what she had to say. And he knew he wouldn't like the rest.

"But we aren't alone. And me in your world, or you in mine... I don't see how that works."

"Malcolm and John and their ladies are happy enough."

"Yes. But they are in a much different station. They are more at liberty to break the rules."

Will opened his mouth to argue but she shook her head. "No, Will, you know I'm right. You saw how it is yourself when you were with Ramsay's men. You were never really trusted, were you? Never quite one of the group. And I've seen how people are since I've been in Scotland. Even at Kirkenroch. The maids stop laughing when I enter the room. They are polite enough, but they make it clear I'm not one of them."

Will frowned, wanting to argue. But she wasn't wrong. Then again, he didn't care if she was wrong or not. He cared only about her.

"They would grow used to ye in time. They'd see ye could be trusted, no matter that ye're an English lass. Or if ye canna bear to be away from yer home, then I'd find a place there."

"In England? Away from your clan, your kin? Philip, John? John can't ever return to England. And Philip...well, he's better off not returning, either. If you wish to remain in their service, then your place is here."

"My place is with ye," he said, smoothing her hair back and drawing her in for a kiss.

"Will," she murmured against his lips.

"No more talking, lass. Let's leave the world behind for a little longer."

She threaded her fingers through his hair and held him fast to her. "Make me forget then, Will. I want to think of only you."

"Yer wish is my command, my lady."

And he spent the next couple hours showing her exactly how wonderful their world together could be.

Chapter Seventeen

Will didn't expect to see anyone for at least another day. Despite Rob's determination to reach Kirkenroch, the lad had been injured. The journey would take a healthy man the better part of a day. So it was with a great deal of surprise, and disappointment, that he heard the sound of a group of men riding toward them.

"Ho there!" someone shouted.

Rose jumped up from where she'd been stirring whatever concoction she'd been planning on force-feeding him and stood, knife in hand, ready to battle whoever disturbed them.

He smiled, his heart breaking a little at the sight of his fierce lass, ready to defend him despite their troubles.

"Looks like the lad made it to Kirkenroch after all," he said, putting a hand on hers to gently lower the dagger.

She glanced up at him, surprised. "It couldn't be him already, could it?"

Will pointed out the door where Rob was pushing through the trees, leading two other men who each led a horse. Will lifted a hand and waved. Then held up a finger to indicate they would be a moment. Rob nodded and conferred with the other men.

Will moved closer to Rose, his body blocking her from view, and bent his head so only she would hear him. "We could tell them to go away. Stay here the rest of our days."

A sad smile touched her lips, and her head bowed. "You would be content with that?"

"If ye were with me? Aye."

She looked at him then, her eyes bright with tears. "Damn you for the devil you are, tempting me with a paradise I cannot have." Her soft smile took away any sting her words might have bestowed. Then she shook her head. "You wouldn't be truly happy. And neither would I."

He frowned and rubbed a thumb across her lips. "Would we no'?"

"In some ways, perhaps. In many ways." That blush he so loved stained her cheeks, and it was all he could do to not pull her into his arms, slam the door, and let the rest of the world be damned.

"But I have my lady," she said. "And you have your laird. And I don't think either of us would rest easy knowing our place should be at their sides."

"Aye." He sighed and hugged her to him. "Well, then. I suppose we should go and let everyone know we yet live."

She hugged him tight, sending bolts of pain shooting through him that he ignored. He'd happily stand in a raging fire if it meant he could feel her touch. She pulled away far too soon and went back into the cottage.

She spent a few minutes gathering up the things she wanted to take back to the manor with them. He stood at the door, simply watching her. If he did nothing else for the rest of his life but watch her, he'd die a happy man.

When they were ready to go, he helped her mount her horse, and it took all his willpower not to mount behind her.

It would be a slow ride back to the manor. One they should probably split over two days, but no one wanted to linger. Even if it meant riding through the night, as long as he could sit a horse, they'd continue on until they reached Kirkenroch's gates.

Part of him wanted to take as much time as possible. Feign weakness and insist on stopping. Truth be told, he wouldn't have to pretend much. His side pulled and burned as if someone were pressing a branding iron to it. But the longer the journey took, the more time he had with Rose before they must part ways for good.

Then again, it would only mean prolonging the pain. No, they couldn't know for sure what Philip and Lady Alice meant to do until they reached the manor. And even then... he still didn't know. His place was at Kirkenroch with John. If John would even have him. And Rose longed for England and her home. Even if Alice were to stay, he didn't think Rose truly wished to.

Facing an unknown future was making his mind spin in dizzying circles. The one constant was the very real possibility he would lose Rose forever. He spurred his horse faster, welcoming the pain that shot through his side. It took his mind off the pain that was rending his heart.

They rode all day, pushing harder than they should. The sun had set hours before and still they'd pressed on. A quarter hour more of hard riding and they would be there. The sooner they reached Kirkenroch, the sooner they could end this torture. One way or the other.

• • •

Rose watched as Will kicked his horse into a run, and she swore under her breath. He'd been keeping them at a brisk pace all day. She would have preferred they take it slow. Savor what time they had left together. And perhaps make it to the manor without undoing all her hard work healing him.

Yet, he hadn't spoken to her since they'd left the cottage. And now it seemed he was so eager to be quit of her that he was willing to break his neck to do it. It was all she could do to keep from urging her horse to follow. Mostly so she could throttle him for endangering himself again. The man was insane. He would probably reopen his wound and bleed to death on the side of the road. It would serve him right.

But the thought still drove a shard of terror straight through her heart. She nudged her horse into a run and followed him, ignoring the startled shouts of Rob and the others.

He turned in the saddle when he heard her coming up behind him, but instead of slowing down, he smiled and spurred his horse faster.

"Idiot," she said, her blood racing. She leaned forward and followed, holding onto her horse for dear life. The others thundered behind her but she ignored them. The only one she cared about was Will. She needed to catch up with him. So she could kill him.

He didn't slow his speed until the manor came into view. She was right behind him as they cantered into the courtyard. Stable hands came out to help with the horses, and a few others went scurrying into the house, most likely to alert the laird and lady of their return. Rose ignored them all. She had eyes for only William, who was dismounting so stiffly it was as if he had a tree branch lodged up his arse.

He dropped to his feet, and she didn't miss the grimace of pain that crossed his face. She didn't wait for help herself but slung her leg over her horse's back and slid down in a flurry of skirts and righteous anger.

His hand held his wounded side as he marched up the stairs leading into the house. He seemed much less steady on his feet than he had yesterday.

"William!" she shouted, her fists clenched at her side.

He ignored her, and she hurried after him.

She stopped just inside the doors to catch her breath. Will kept making his way through the Great Hall toward the staircase that led to the family's quarters.

"William!" she shouted again.

He stopped this time and turned, looking at her expectantly as if she hadn't been chasing him for the better part of an hour.

"Are you out of your mind?" she asked, marching toward him. "What were you thinking? Are you trying to get yourself killed? I can't believe you—"

She stopped short, belatedly realizing she'd stormed past Laird John and Lady Elizabet.

"I'm so sorry, my lord, my lady." She dropped a quick curtsy. "I…"

John had his arms crossed across his chest but looked absolutely delighted with the whole situation, beaming at them both. Lady Elizabet looked just as amused. She simply smiled and said, "Don't mind us. You and he…" She waved Rose toward William.

"Agreed," John said. "By all means, continue."

Rose frowned, a bit confused but honestly too worked up about Will's foolhardiness to focus on them too much. She turned back to Will who scowled at John.

"Dinna start with me, cousin," he said. "There's nothing to be amused at. And there's certainly nothing to be concerned about so dinna encourage her—"

That snapped Rose out of her momentary confusion. "Nothing to be concerned about? With you bleeding all over their floor?"

Will glanced down at his shirt, which was indeed stained with blood. He scowled. "Och, it's naught—"

"Don't you *it's naught* me," Rose said. "I didn't spend almost a month saving your life so you could kill yourself within two minutes of arriving home. Now sit down," she said, pointing to a chair near the hearth. Then she pointed at one of the people who had gathered to stare at them, mouths agape. "You, fetch me some water and clean cloths and something I can use for a bandage."

He didn't move until she rounded on him, hands on her hips. Then he held up his hands in surrender, a bemused expression on his face that had her both softening toward him and wanting to throttle him at the same time.

"Sit," she ordered.

He sank into the chair and she got to work tending him, muttering under her breath the whole time.

She vaguely noticed John and Elizabet sitting nearby, clearly waiting for explanations. But she ignored everyone while she knelt by his side and redressed his wounds. Once she was done, she sat back on her heels and raised a trembling hand to brush a few strands of hair from her face.

It seemed like the last month was finally catching up to her. She wanted to laugh and cry and scream and curse. And, since she could do none of those things, she sat and trembled, trying to focus on breathing.

"Rose," Will said, in the same soft and caring voice he used only when they were alone together.

She wouldn't look up at him. Couldn't. Or she'd lose what little composure she had managed to maintain.

"Why did you do that?" she asked, hating how small her voice sounded. "Why did you rush so quickly to return that you reinjured yourself? Do you really hate me so much?"

"Oh, Rose." He took her chin between his fingers and tilted her face up so she had to look at him. "I could never hate ye. Quite the opposite. I just want the torture to end."

She pulled her face from his grasp with a mirthless laugh.

"I know we don't get along, but torture is a bit strong a word, isn't it?" She shook her head and stood, but he followed and caught her hand before she could leave.

"That's no' what I meant. We couldna ken anything until we got back home. We didna ken how matters stood here, with Philip and his lady, and the rest. So I simply wanted to get here."

"Will," she said, shaking her head. "We've discussed this. My place is back in London with Lady Alice, yours with your laird. Even if they choose to remain together…"

"Aye, ye've told me. Ye're English, I'm Scottish. I dinna care. I dinna think ye really do either. It's an excuse because ye're too scared."

"Scared? Me?"

"Aye. You. What would ye say if Lady Alice walked in right now and told ye that she was madly in love with Philip and staying here for the rest of her days?"

Rose frowned, her heart thumping painfully. What would she say? Part of her would be shouting for joy. But yes, another part was terrified.

"See?" he said, triumphantly. "Even the mere thought of no obstacles makes ye frown and chew yer lip."

"Do you really think we'd have no obstacles even if Lady Alice were to stay? We can't even go an hour without fighting like cats and dogs."

"Aye, and ye love every second of it. Next?"

"I do not love every second of it."

Except, she definitely did. But was that any way to have a relationship?

He snorted, which she ignored. "And besides," she said, "Even if Lady Alice remains here, that doesn't mean she's staying with Philip, and if she does, that doesn't mean they will live here. What if they wish to travel the continent or move to London or…?"

She frowned, looking around. "Where is Lady Alice?"

Elizabet smiled and waved at them. "As I've been trying to say…"

Rose blushed furiously, only now realizing Lady Elizabet had been trying to say something for several minutes now.

"My pardon, my lady," Rose said.

Elizabet waved her apology away. "I hated to interrupt, but I do have some information that might make a difference. Alice and Philip *are* staying together. They left here not long ago to sail for London."

"London?" Will said with a slight frown.

Rose turned to him, an icy ball of despair already forming in her heart. Her lady had returned home without her. She should follow. Immediately. Her place was with Lady Alice and to be home again… She missed it dreadfully. But she would miss Scotland, too. And some parts of it—she stared at William—she'd never get over leaving.

He took a deep breath and straightened, giving her a slow, steady smile that pierced straight through to her soul. Then he took her hand and led her over to John.

"I pledged ye my loyalty and service, but I must ask yer leave to return to London."

John's eyes widened in surprise, and Rose gasped. "What are you doing?" she asked, pulling on his hand. But he only drew her in to his side and tucked her arm against him, holding their clasped hands up to his lips for a kiss before resting them on his chest, above his heart.

He pressed another kiss to her forehead and then leaned closer to whisper to her. "I love ye with everything that I am, my darling Rose. Thorns and all."

He looked back to John. "My Rose's place is at her lady's side. And my place is with Rose. If she must return to London, then I wish to go with her."

"Will," Rose said, a sob catching in her throat. "You

don't have to do this."

"Aye, I do, lass. And I'm glad to do it." He laughed, genuine happiness beaming from his face. "It's the first decision I've ever made that I'm no' afraid will backfire in my face." He stroked a thumb across her cheek. "Ye'll always be my best decision."

Elizabet clasped her hands together and leaned against her husband. "That is the most romantic thing I've ever heard," she said, wiping at her suddenly teary eyes. Then she laughed. "I'm sorry. After the baby, everything seems to make me so emotional."

John laughed and patted his wife's back. "Will, ye're free to go wherever ye'd like. And I'd be sad to see ye go, certainly, but—"

Will didn't let him finish. He turned to Rose. "Marry me, lass."

Rose sucked in a breath and then let it out with a laugh. She didn't know whether to cry for joy or smack some sense into him. "We can't get married just like that."

"Why not?"

"We've known each other only a short time."

"Aye. And?"

She shook her head. "You're mad."

"Well, I love ye, so aye, that seems apt."

Her mouth dropped open, and he laughed again. She crossed her arms and shook her head. "If I say yes, we'll probably both regret it the rest of our lives."

"Why? Because we canna go an hour without fighting?"

"To begin with."

He pulled her to him so quickly she yelped in surprise and held onto him for dear life. He nuzzled her neck, whispering so only she could hear. "Aye, but after the fighting comes the loving. The fighting just gives it a bit more passion, aye?"

That startled a laugh out of her, and her cheeks flamed.

She pulled back so she could look into his eyes. "Is this really what you want? Am I?"

He smiled down at her. "More than anything."

"Even if you have to live in London to have me?"

"Even if I have to spend my days licking old King Charlie's boots."

She shook her head and cupped his face. "Well, hopefully it won't come to that."

He raised a brow. "Is that a yes, then?"

She took a deep breath and slowly let it out. "Go find a reverend."

His smile took her breath away. Then he picked her up and spun her around, and she swatted at him. "Put me down, you madman! You'll start bleeding again."

"I dinna care," he said, though he lowered her back to the floor. Slowly. Letting her feel every inch of him as he did so.

"*I* care," she said, staying on her toes so she could press a soft kiss to his lips.

Someone cleared a throat and Rose and Will looked over at a weepy but smiling Elizabet and a very amused John.

"We are thrilled for ye both. However..." John started.

But Elizabet burst in before he could finish. "You don't need to go anywhere! Unless their plans change, Alice and Philip are planning on returning once Alice sees to her sister. And they will be staying here at Kirkenroch."

Will just blinked at them and then burst out laughing. Rose joined in, wrapping her arms around his waist.

He cupped her face in his hands and gazed down at her. "Will ye stay here with me, then?"

"Yes."

"Ye ken I mean Scotland when I say *here*? Because I meant it. We can return to London, if ye wish."

"Scotland has a few things I've grown to love," she said, reaching up to kiss him. "Now let's go find that reverend."

His laughter rang through the hall and her heart, filling her with joy. She'd been so afraid she'd miss her home or afraid he'd resent her for having to leave his.

But he *was* her home. And she was his. As long as they were together, the rest would fall into place.

They were home now.

Acknowledgments

Thank you so much to my readers! You guys make it possible for me to do what I love, and I love each and every one of you. Massive thanks to my amazing editor, Erin Molta, without whom I'd be truly lost. Toni and Sarah, you two are my rocks. Thank you for keeping me sane. Well, mostly sane. To the amazing team at Entangled, thank you so much for all the time and effort you put into making each of my books a success! And to my family, I love you so much. Thank you for your everlasting support and for putting up with your deadline-crazed mama.

About the Author

Romance and nonfiction author Michelle McLean is a jeans and T-shirt kind of girl who is addicted to chocolate and Goldfish crackers and spent most of her formative years with her nose in a book. She has a B.S. in History, a M.A. in English, loves history and romance, and enjoys spending her time combining the two in her novels.

When Michelle's not editing, reading, or chasing her kids around, she can usually be found in a quiet corner working on her next book. She resides in Pennsylvania with her husband and two children, a massively overgrown puppy, two crazy parakeets, and three very spoiled cats. She also writes contemporary romance as Kira Archer.

Get Scandalous with these historical reads...

HIS REBELLIOUS LASS
a *Scottish Hearts* novel by Callie Hutton

When Lord Campbell inherits a Scottish beauty as his ward, it's his job to marry her off. Easy. Lady Bridget will have plenty of suitors. But Bridget has plans for that fortune and she refuses to help her handsome guardian find her a husband. Bridget and Cam are on opposite sides of a war that neither one plans to lose. Even if neither can deny that they set each other's heart afire. And then Cam makes a bold proposal...

HIGHLAND SALVATION
a *Highland Pride* novel by Lori Ann Bailey

Finlay Cameron weds stunning Blair Macnab to ensure her clan's loyalty. She's everything he's ever wanted, but she may be plotting his murder. Always considered nothing but a pretty face, Blair Macnab refuses to be used as a political pawn, but when confronted by a blackmailer, she marries the brawny Finlay Cameron to escape. But her blackmailer is hot on her trail and her secrets could soon be exposed...

TEMPTING THE HIGHLAND SPY
a *Highland Hearts* novel by Tara Kingston

It had been one glorious night, and Harrison MacMasters, Highland spy, never thought to see jewel thief Grace Winters again. Now he's forced to protect her as they join together to catch a killer, even though he can't trust her with anything, especially his heart. Grace will do anything to keep her family from the poorhouse, including a pretend marriage to the one man who tempts her to make it real.

THE SCOTTISH ROGUE
a *Campbells* novel by Heather McCollum

Englishwoman Evelyn Worthington is resolved to build a school for ladies in her brother's Scottish castle. But when she arrives, she finds the castle scorched by fire, and a brawny Highlander bars her entry. Clan chief Grey Campbell would rather die than see Finlarig Castle fall into English hands. After secrets are revealed, the fates of the Campbell Clan, the school, and a possible future for Grey and Evelyn are in as much jeopardy as their lives.

Printed in the USA
CPSIA information can be obtained
at www.ICGtesting.com
LVHW032202310723
753995LV00027B/229

9 781078 046589